Conversations
with a
4,000-Year-Old Fungus

Conversations with a 4,000-Year-Old Fungus

John Bonnell

|IX|

The Ninth Measure

ISBN 979-8-9956123-0-8 (Paperback)

Cover art and book design by John Bonnell

Published by The Ninth Measure

johnbonnell.com

To you-know-who, for you-know-what

Contents

The Value of Perseverance

Smack!

The little bird stumbled and staggered around, dazed and panting. He breathed heavily. The world spun, then slowly the views in both eyes leveled out and became one again.

Back up to the tree branch he flew.

He dove off, flapped his wings, gained speed—

Smack!

The titmouse lay on the ground a while, motionless and stunned.

When he regained his senses, he flew back to the branch.

"Hey!" said someone, just as the bird was about to launch himself off again.

"Huh?" said the little titmouse, blearily.

"What the hell are you doing?"

The titmouse looked around. It was one of the local squirrels clinging upside down to the tree trunk.

"What do you mean?" said the bird.

"*What do I mean?*" responded the squirrel, harshly. "You're repeatedly flying into that window over there. What are you, nuts?—hmm, I gotta find some nuts in a minute." He looked around, flicking his tail.

"Uh? Window?"

"Yeah, that window. Over there." He swished his tail disapprovingly.

"I honestly don't know what you're talking about. I've simply been trying to fly through that hole over there, where the light is coming from, but I keep hitting something. It pops up in front of me so fast I can't stop in time. I have no idea what it is."

"Yeah. That's called a window. There's no hole there."

"Sure there is. I can see the sunlight just beyond it."

"No, there isn't—oh crap!" The squirrel zipped around the tree, popped his head back into view, then zipped back to where he had been. "Whew, thought I saw something. Anyway, you're all messed up."

"What do you mean?"

"Quit saying that. I told you, there is *no* hole there."

"Sure there is—"

"No. It's a window."

"What's a window?"

"Okay," said the squirrel, thinking for a moment. "Let's see. It's an invisible barrier. It *looks* like a hole, but it isn't."

"Wow," said the little bird, "that's amazing. I've never heard of such a thing."

"Obviously."

"Well, you don't need to get all snippy."

"I'm not the one flying into windows."

Before the titmouse could say anything, the squirrel zipped up the tree, jumping from one branch to another, then to the next tree and on out of sight.

The titmouse considered what the squirrel had told him.

"Invisible barriers," said the titmouse to himself. "That doesn't sound very plausible. Must be the wind blowing something in my path."

He thought about it for a moment.

"That makes more sense," he said to himself.

He stretched his wings and fluffed his feathers, securing his footing on the tree branch. He double-checked the wind currents and plotted his trajectory. Everything was perfect.

Down he swooped.

Smack!

Perspectives

"Hi, I'm a chameleon, and I have a really long tongue. Surprisingly, nobody is as impressed by this as I am."

"I'm a cute, fluffy bun—"

"I'm a wolf. And I like rabbits."

"Howdy, I am a cow. I think that says it all."

"I carry my nuts to and fro. I'm the wee squirrel."

"I'm a marmoset. I'm a monkey!"

"Hello, uh . . . I'm a, er . . . dung beetle. And, well . . . I roll shit around all day. No, really."

Dissension in the Animal Kingdom

"So," said the rabbit, twitching his cute little nose, "you're trying to tell me there's some sort of alien creature running around through the woods?"

"Yes," said the weasel. "It's really big and ferocious. Look out!"

Too late. The rabbit was quickly devoured by the fox.

"Hah!" said the fox. "That's such a cool trick. Let's do it again tomorrow."

"Sure thing."

The two animals parted ways. The weasel went off through the bushes while the fox trotted off between the trees.

"What are you up to, foxy?" asked the owl from a high branch.

The fox stopped and looked up. It took him a minute to zero in on the source of the query.

"Oh, hey. Just eating rabbits—the usual."

"I hear you have quite the scam going with the weasel. Not very sporting, I'd say."

"You're a fine one to talk. You just sit up there and wait for things to pop their unsuspecting heads up, then you swoop down and nab 'em."

"But they know the danger. It's familiar. It's the natural order of things. What you're doing is just mean."

"So, what are you going to do about it? You eat the same things I do. Oh, I get it—you want a piece of the action. Well—"

"Wait a minute. I don't want any part of it. And as for what I'm going to do—well, I don't know yet."

"Yeah, whatever."

The fox continued on his way to nowhere in particular.

The next day, the fox was waiting patiently in the bushes. The weasel had a little mouse locked in a spine-tingling tale about three-headed monsters with flaming nostrils. A few minutes later, there was one less mouse in the world.

"That went well," said the fox.

"Yeah, that one was priceless," said the weasel.

From high on a branch, the owl watched disapprovingly.

"Distasteful," he muttered, swallowing the last of the chipmunk he'd caught moments earlier.

The Snoofer

"What was that?" asked Mrs. Johnson.

"I'll go find out," said Mr. Johnson, slowly working his way out of the overstuffed chair.

He opened the back door and looked out, but he didn't see anything. Not that there was much to see in the dark, even with the moon shining as brightly as it was. He listened. Nothing. Then more clanking. The trash cans. He couldn't see those either thanks to the wooden privacy fence he had recently installed. He closed the door and went to get his flashlight.

"I think it's a cat or something poking around in the trash. I'll run it off."

"All right," said Mrs. Johnson, following him to the back door.

Mr. Johnson made his way to the gate and then stepped out into the alley. His flashlight scanned the area left and right, but its beam landed on nothing unusual. The trash cans were still upright. Then he noticed that the lids were lying on the ground. *Damn cats*, he thought to himself. But then he realized that cats probably wouldn't have simply knocked the lids off. Could they even? He wondered.

He took a look inside the nearest can and was surprised to find it empty. Completely empty. The other can, too, was empty. Someone must have come along and stolen his trash. That was the only explanation, since trash pick up was not until morning. Why anyone would steal trash was beyond him. But he knew it happened. People were even known to attempt to extort money from the former owners of the trash. It was mind-boggling. He checked up and down the alley again for any suspicious characters. But no one was about.

He decided to head back in and started for the gate when he heard a *clang* behind him. Spinning around, he aimed the flashlight and saw one of his neighbor's trash can lids lying on the ground.

Curiosity overcame him as he approached his neighbor's trash cans, but he jumped back when his light set upon what appeared to be a huge snake slithering over the far edge of the trash can and down inside. Running back into the house was a thought that crossed his mind a number of times in only a fraction of a second. He shook off the shivers that ran down his body, and shone the light back on the snake.

Or was it a snake? Something wasn't right about it. Probing around inside the can as it was just didn't seem natural. And it must be a big snake indeed, for it was still hanging over the far edge of the trash can.

While he was considering his next move he was startled yet again. This time by a peculiar sound. It was like someone had just sucked a small elephant through a vacuum cleaner nozzle—a stifled *whoosh* followed by a triumphant *whoomp*. There was a tinny echo from the metal trash can.

The snake withdrew from the can. But it wasn't a snake. It was more of a hose. It nudged the other trash can's lid off. The lid flipped up and landed on the ground with a *clank*. The hose slithered over the edge of the can and began probing around again.

Mr. Johnson elected to investigate further. How could he not? The thought really didn't even cross his mind as he drew closer to the cans.

He aimed the light around the nearer trash can, and what he saw was something he had simply never seen before. It was a strange sight, and he just didn't know how to react to it.

Attached to the hose was some sort of creature. A cross between an anteater and a giant bumblebee, with four stubby legs, large round eyes, and the hose, or rather, its long hose-like nose. Its coat was vertically striped, multicolored, and fuzzy.

Mr. Johnson took a step backwards, tripped over something, and fell on his ass.

He quickly propped himself up and shone the flashlight back on the creature. Its huge eyes glared at him, and it withdrew its long proboscis from the can. Mr. Johnson scrambled to his feet as the nose was directed at him and began sniffing.

He jumped back, and ended up flat against the fence on the other side of the alley, his head searching uncontrollably for a direction of egress.

As the creature came ever closer Mr. Johnson became frozen in place when the long nose reached out and sniffed at his crotch. He hadn't even seen it coming, for all of his attention was focused on the body and the huge eyes. He decided to make a mad dash, but tripped again, this time landing on his chest. He just lay there as the creature walked the two feet to his head.

A tongue reached out and licked his face.

He blinked.

He was licked again.

He blinked again, then slowly rolled over.

The creature was staring at him. He returned the stare. It licked him again.

Mr. Johnson relaxed, a little, and reached out to pet the creature. It didn't resist the attempt; in fact, it seemed to enjoy it quite a bit. It snuggled up against him.

He continued to pet it, while slowly working it off of himself so he could stand up. It didn't seem to be upset in any way. In fact, it seemed very happy to be with someone. If it had had a tail, he was sure it would be wagging it uncontrollably.

After he had brushed himself off a bit, Mr. Johnson got to wondering about the trash again. He looked in his neighbor's trash cans, and just like his own, they were empty. He looked at the little creature, and in the voice one uses to talk to babies and animals he said, "You didn't eat all of that garbage did you?"

The little creature only looked up and wagged its nonexistent tail. It was clear it had ingested the garbage, even if it defied common sense; the creature was only about knee high, after all.

By this time Mrs. Johnson was getting worried. She had been watching from inside the back door. But now she saw Mr. Johnson coming back through the gate. But what was that following him? She couldn't make it out clearly: some kind of animal? He didn't bring home some stray, did he? She hoped not.

As Mr. Johnson entered the house, he was obviously excited. Mrs. Johnson hastened to wonder what that meant.

"I have found the most amazing creature," he said. "Now, don't be alarmed, it's not something you've ever seen before." He let the creature inside.

Mrs. Johnson screeched, "What is it?!"

In the full light of the house, the true brilliance of the animal's coat could be seen. Its body was ringed with bands of red, white, pink, green, and a few other colors no one could identify, all flowing together very subtly, yet distinctly separate. Mrs. Johnson wasn't sure whether to faint or hit it with the broom. She elected to stand nonplussed as a happy medium.

"Well," said Mr. Johnson, "I don't really know." He put the flashlight down on the counter. "All I know is that it's friendly, it eats garbage, and it's going to solve all of our problems. Or, at the very least, it will save us money on trash collection." He smiled.

Mrs. Johnson, for the moment, was not completely impressed.

Mr. Johnson said, "Here, watch this." He got some bananas and threw the peels into the kitchen garbage can. Then dug around under the sink and found a few half-empty cans of bug spray, paint, and some other junk he didn't know was there, and tossed it all into the garbage can as well. He threw in a few paper towels for good measure. Mrs. Johnson watched as he then went to the refrigerator and pulled out the leftover casserole from the evening meal. "Let's be honest dear," he said, grinning. He tossed that in too.

He shook the plastic garbage can around to mix it all up, then he pushed in the lid-flap, and said, "Here little fella, come and get it."

The couple watched as the little creature hopped over to the trash can and extended its long nose through the opening. After a few seconds of probing, there was a *snoof* and the appendage was withdrawn. The creature seemed rather content and walked over to a corner and lay down.

"See, the garbage is gone. The creature ate it. Or 'snoofed' it, or whatever."

Mrs. Johnson cautiously looked in the can. And, sure enough, the garbage was gone, bag and all.

She was amazed.

"That's probably what I looked like when I saw it," said Mr. Johnson.

They looked at the little creature; it was sleeping peacefully in the corner. "I guess it had its fill," said Mr. Johnson.

After a brief discussion of whether it was a good idea, the Johnsons went off to bed, leaving the creature to sleep in the kitchen. They would decide what exactly was to be done with it in the morning.

★ ★ ★

The alarm rang out, the sun shone through the curtains, and a new day had begun. When the Johnsons went to the kitchen they found the little creature pawing at the back door. It clearly wanted out, so they obliged it. At least it was house trained, they thought.

They watched as the creature walked around their backyard for a few minutes. Then it got a pained look on its face, and out of its bottom popped a stuffed animal. A bear, they thought.

They were astonished. Then, a few seconds later, out popped a quilt. Then what looked like a wicker basket. This sequence of events continued a few more times, and then the creature headed back toward the house.

"This thing is even more amazing than I had first thought," said Mr. Johnson. Mrs. Johnson was clearly just as astonished, and nodded in agreement.

The two of them went out to look over what the little creature had just excreted. And what they found were the most skillfully crafted works they had ever seen. The quilts were of the finest quality and the stitching was perfect. The stuffed bears were of the same high standard. And the wicker baskets, well, normal wicker baskets could only hope to be so good.

Mr. Johnson reached down and petted the little creature who dutifully enjoyed it. "Good boy—er, or whatever you are," he said.

They collected the bounty and went back in for breakfast.

Later, Mrs. Johnson was folding the quilts while Mr. Johnson placed the stuffed bears into the baskets. At least cleaning up the mess was a fun activity. And potentially profitable too, Mr. Johnson thought. He had had another idea after breakfast. And this was even better than the last one.

"You know," he said, "we should set up a booth at one of those crafts markets you're always bringing junk home from. We could sell this stuff and make some extra money."

"It's not junk."

Mr. Johnson smiled to himself.

Mrs. Johnson said, "But that is a good idea. These things are very well made."

"Especially considering where they came from."

"Stop it," she said.

The little creature nestled itself against Mr. Johnson's leg, and took a little nap.

Mr. Johnson reached down and gave it a gentle pat on the back.

But now Mr. Johnson was getting curious about just where this creature had come from. It was obviously a peaceful animal—if animal was the correct term for it. It certainly didn't seem like a very naturally occurring animal; at least, not for earth.

Mr. Johnson chuckled to himself at the thought of it being an alien from space.

Maybe it was just an experiment escaped from some lab or something. So far there had been no news of such an incident. Though there probably wouldn't be. It didn't seem like the sort of thing anyone would want others to know about.

And the creature certainly had an appetite for refuse. In fact, that seemed to be its only dietary intake. This would, however, save money on pet food.

But, regardless of the particulars, he was intent on keeping it. It would make a fine pet after all, and then there was its money making potential.

★ ★ ★

The creature became like one of the family: When Mrs. Johnson was fixing a meal, the Snoofer, as it had come to be called, sat next to the sink and snoofed up any garbage that was produced in the process of cooking. During the day, it swept the floors for anything that it found appealing—it seemed to know just what was garbage and what wasn't.

It was very happy to receive attention from the Johnsons. Mr. Johnson even taught the little creature some tricks.

And every morning it produced more quilts, bears, and baskets. All in assorted colors and styles.

Once a week, the couple took their creature-produced knickknacks to the local crafts market where comments like "My goodness, where did you find the time to make such beautiful things" were often overheard.

The stuff sold wildly; people came from all over to get either a quilt, a bear, or a basket—or all three packaged together. In a few months the Johnsons had made quite a lot of money.

"We have all of this money now, let's go on a vacation," said Mrs. Johnson to her husband.

He agreed that it was a very good idea.

So, the Johnsons prepared to go on a weeklong vacation, and they thought about what to do with the Snoofer. They couldn't take it with them; its strange appearance would simply attract too much attention. And they couldn't put it in a kennel, for the same reason. Since it was used to living in the house most of the time already, they decided they would just lock it up inside while they were away, leaving a few containers of garbage here and there for it to munch on. They knew that what it produced wouldn't be a problem.

In the morning, they petted the little creature goodbye, and went on their way.

Over the past few months they had put so much time into marketing crafts that they really needed a break. They decided to fly to Hawaii for the week, where they could enjoy the weather and have a nice relaxing trip.

While on the flight, Mr. Johnson read an article in the newspaper he brought along about a glowing pod that was found near his home, but he didn't really find it all that interesting.

★ ★ ★

At first the Snoofer was content, and snoofed up some of the nice garbage the Johnsons had left for it. A few hours later, however, when no one had returned, it began to wonder where everyone had gone. It pawed at the door for a while, not really wanting out, but not really wanting to stay in either. It did what it felt it had to do.

But there was more snoofing to do. And soon the Snoofer had snoofed all of the garbage that had been left for it and was in dire need of something else to intake. That is what Snoofers did, after all—they snoofed.

It jumped around nervously, looking for something that might pass for garbage, but it could find nothing that could be deemed suitable. It lay down and tried to make the best of it.

By the end of the day it was very hungry for something to snoof; it eyed the trash can with lust. Every fiber of its being was telling it not to. But it had to snoof something. It extended its proboscis cautiously—looking around as if to see if anyone was watching—then *snoof* went the trash can.

It felt bad; this was somehow wrong.

But it wasn't satisfied.

Then it remembered what Mr. Johnson had done when it had first arrived. And, using its long nose, it opened the door under the sink, probing around inside before it sucked in whatever it had found.

This satisfied it, for now.

But the next day it awoke famished.

It thought about the refrigerator. But when opened, it revealed little of snoofable value. Under the circumstances, however, it snoofed the stuff anyway.

This paltry meal was not enough.

It felt abandoned. But it felt hungry too. The latter won out in its struggle of things to think about.

It started searching for other things to snoof.

Considering the limited palette available, the little Snoofer would just have to widen its sense of what counted as trash.

Mrs. Johnson had recently brought home an old lamp which she had found in an antiques shoppe, and the Snoofer looked at it carefully. A few seconds later the lamp was gone.

After the lamp went the chair next to it. What good was the lamp without the chair, it thought.

This was getting easier.

It slept contentedly that night.

The next morning, the ratty old sofa went too.

By the end of the day, so did the beds and the pictures on the walls.

★ ★ ★

A few days later, the Johnsons returned home. And as they opened the door they saw the Snoofer suck in the TV, followed by the stereo, and then the shelves the whole mess had been sitting on.

They stood aghast in the doorway. All they could see were quilts and stuffed bears piled indiscriminately inside their home. The ravenous little creature looked their way. It had a very wild look in its huge eyes. It wasn't a malicious look, but rather a look of desperation.

It took this opportunity to bolt outside through the open door.

The Johnsons had never seen it move so fast before.

They watched as it sucked in their car; then the neighbor's flowers; then the neighbor's car. They didn't know what to do. Standing awestruck was all they could manage for the moment.

The little Snoofer bounded off down the street, snoofing up anything that got in its path; with quilts and bears popping out every now and again.

The Johnsons slowly regained their senses, walking up the street looking for the creature, but the little Snoofer was gone. They gave up and went home.

The couple stood at the threshold to their house for only a brief few seconds before entering. Inside it was packed with the plush excrement of the Snoofer. All of the furniture was gone, as was everything else.

They looked at each other and shrugged, then they smiled. They dropped the armloads of quilts, bears, and baskets they had collected on the walk back to the house.

They slept contentedly that night knowing that their immediate future had been secured thanks to the droppings of a small, oddly shaped creature.

That's One Fat Monkey

Jimmy was the fattest monkey in the world. He was fed well by his captors; banana mush, banana purée, and bananas that were just squished up. He lived in a cage at the university, and passersby would say things like, "Damn, that's the fattest monkey I've ever seen." This sort of thing didn't bother Jimmy—he was, after all, just a monkey. And just what kind of monkey, no one was sure anymore. Originally, he had been a howler monkey, but he had gotten so fat they had to rename his species.

One day, after much lack of thought, Jimmy escaped. He didn't get very far, though—he was so fat, he could barely move. Ten feet from the cage, it was estimated. In some fit of wisdom, someone realized this wasn't very healthy for Jimmy. And so it was decided that the monkey should lose some weight.

They brought in a trainer, a forklift, a motivational speaker, two female monkeys, an ice chest full of cans of diet soda, twenty-four popular workout videos, a large sound system, stacks of pornographic magazines, and—well, that was it, really.

In fourteen weeks, Jimmy—the fattest monkey in the world—was reduced to the size of a normal howler monkey, at which time his keepers discovered that Jimmy was, in fact, an orangutan. How someone could have made the mistake in the first place, no one knew. But it had been made, and now someone would have to pay for it.

And that someone was a fellow by the name of Carl Fornswallow.

Carl was an odd, unassuming man, seemingly always in a white lab coat and often seen carrying a clipboard. It was on this day—the day of the "Great Discovery"—that Carl was walking along the campus, in his lab coat and carrying his clipboard, on his way to do something he felt was very important. He had a little project he was working on, and it had to do with melting ice. It wasn't very interesting to most people, so he didn't talk about it much.

"Carl," shouted someone from somewhere.

Carl turned and saw his friend Mike.

"Hello, Mike," said Carl, walking up to his friend.

"Have you heard the news?" said Mike.

"What news?"

"Somebody blew it with Jimmy the fat monkey. He's really an orangutan."

Carl's eyes widened in surprise. "Now that's something."

"That's not all. You're going to have to appear at a press conference to explain it."

"What!" The usually subdued man, almost, but not quite, dropped his clipboard.

"Yeah. Come on, it starts in five minutes. We've got to get you on stage."

"Wait a minute. I don't know anything about—"

Mike grabbed Carl by the arm and led him along to the little room where the media had gathered. Some brawny security types helped the reluctant speaker to the podium.

"I don't—" started Carl, as the questions flew fast and furious at him.

"I—" It went on like this for some time, and when it was over, Carl was unceremoniously booted out of his job. And that was that. Oh, he whined a bit about his ice-melting project and threatened to sue, so the higher-ups brought him back after everything had calmed down and gave him a nice grant and everything.

Life likewise returned more or less to normal for Jimmy. He couldn't be allowed to stay the size of a howler monkey anymore than he could be allowed to become so fat he couldn't move. Proper dietary plans were drawn up and put into action, a regular exercise regimen was implemented, appropriate music was played over the sound system, new pornographic magazines were purchased, and a lot of diet soda was consumed.

Soon, Jimmy made his target weight and maintained it. Of course, he could no longer be called the fattest monkey in the world—he technically wasn't even a monkey. But Jimmy didn't mind. He was a renewed ape, with adoring fans, a laminated gym pass, more energy, and still more determination.

And the next time he escaped, he made it all the way to the vending machines.

Squirrels

Someday, squirrels could rule the universe. Don't think it couldn't hap-pen. All it takes is one squirrel who can look beyond his own horizons.

"Hey Joe," said Mike, flicking his tail back and forth, "what's with this whole nut thing?"

"What do you mean?" said Joe, clinging upside down to the side of the tree.

"I mean, we gather nuts, right? And then we bury them. Sometimes we pee on the spot. Then later we dig 'em up. There has to be more to life."

Joe looked at his friend on the tree branch and said, "Like what?"

"Something. I'm not sure yet. I'll work on it."

The two squirrels went back to nut gathering. They fol-lowed the well-worn path back to the spot where the nuts had fallen. Then they retraced the path once more to the place they would bury the nuts.

"Okay," said Mike, "I've got it. You see that big thing that the giants get into? The one that moves around."

"Yeah," said Joe.

"We're going to take control of it."

"How?"

"Don't worry, I have a plan."

The friends climbed the tree beside the big thing the giants used, the one that moved around, and out onto the branch above it. There they waited.

"How long is this going to take?" asked Joe.

"I don't know," said Mike, "but give it a while longer."

"All right."

A short time later, two giants emerged from the big thing that didn't move around and got into the big thing that did. The thing roared.

"Now!" said Mike, leaping onto the top of the thing. Joe put all thoughts of sanity behind him and leapt after his friend.

The big thing started to move.

"Hold on to something," said Mike.

There were some branch-like things to hold on to, so they grasped them tightly as the big thing roared and sped away.

Jimbob the Great

The castle loomed in the distance as Jimbob the Great raised his sword high above his head. He was tall and thin, short-haired, and in his early twenties. "Hey, Momma," he yelled, "look at this." He twirled the sword round and round. Then it abruptly flew out of his hand, arced through the air, and stuck itself in the ground next to the hulking JoBilly.

"Hah!" cried Jimbob.

"Now you boys quit showin' off," called Jeanie May, Jimbob's mother, from the door of the longhouse.

"Okay, Momma." Jimbob jerked his sword out of the ground. "Let's go kill us something, JoBilly."

The large man nodded and grabbed his shield and sword.

Off they went: down the hill; through the forest; past the old stone circle; up the other hill; in the cave; out the cave; down the hole; and back to the surface.

"Damn, JoBilly," said Jimbob, "you stink. Didn't you go down and bathe like Momma told you?"

JoBilly nodded that he had.

"You're gonna ruin our reputation smellin' like that. And I think you're scarin' off all the big critters."

JoBilly sniffed his tunic and shrugged.

"Hail, Jimbob," called Sir Richard of Flittindam, riding up on his large white horse. The blue and yellow coat of arms emblazoned on his surcoat stood out boldly against the green of the surrounding foliage. "What would you two rapscallions be up to today?"

"Hey, Richie," said Jimbob. "Just out lookin' for some beast to kill."

Sir Richard smiled. "You are truly a great slayer of beasts."

"Thanks. You boys sure did some fine work on the castle."

"You must dine with us some evening in the new hall. I know of a fair maid that has her eye on your brother."

JoBilly smiled.

"Hey, you know we'll be there," said Jimbob, grinning broadly and elbowing his brother in the side.

"I must be on my way, friends," said Sir Richard. "The burdens of politics are never-ending."

"See ya, Richie."

"Good day. And good hunting." Sir Richard rode off down the trail.

"Hell," said Jimbob, "let's go to town."

★ ★ ★

Once in town, they bought some ale and headed home.

Halfway home, Jimbob stopped and sniffed the air. "I smell somethin'," he said. Then a large, pale-skinned ogre jumped out from behind a tree and pounced on him.

JoBilly dropped the large skin of ale and knocked the ogre off of his brother by putting all of his weight behind his shield.

The ogre rolled and sliced JoBilly with its sharp claws as they both hit the ground.

Jimbob sprang to his feet and swung his sword down on the beast's head, cracking its skull.

"That's why they call me Jimbob the Great!"

JoBilly stood up.

"You OK?" asked Jimbob.

The large man nodded, wiping the blood from his leg.

"Hah," said Jimbob, "we best get on home. Momma can make herself a fine new dress out this thing's hide. I'll grab the ale—you drag this critter home."

The boys drank their ale that night and skinned the ogre. In a few weeks, Jeanie May had herself a fancy new dress that she proudly showed off while shopping at the market. It wasn't long before Jimbob's three cousins wanted new ogre-skin dresses, too. He did his best to oblige.

The Red Rug
of
My Discontent

As Dick unloaded the small red rug from his delivery truck, another truck pulled up and parked next to him. It was Bill. Dick stopped and stared. Something was clearly amiss.

Bill got out of his truck and went around to the rear.

"Hey, Dick," said Bill carelessly. "What are you doing here?"

"What do you mean?" asked Dick, feeling rather perplexed. "It's my day."

"No it isn't."

"Sure it is. You were here last time."

"I was not."

The two men stared intently at each other for a minute in front of the gift shoppe.

Finally, Bill spoke. "You've been taking those classes again, haven't you?" he said.

"What classes?"

"Those 'How to be a pain in the ass' classes."

Dick's face showed his surprise at the comment.

Bill turned away, retrieving a rug from his truck.

"What the hell are you going to do with that?" said Dick. "It's my day. I've got the new rug right here."

"Yeah, well, we'll just see about that." He advanced on the shoppe.

The gauntlet had been thrown down.

"I can't let you do that," said Dick, standing his ground between the taller and heavier Bill and the shoppe.

Bill tried to go around, but couldn't find an open corridor.

"You're not getting in there," said Dick with calm conviction.

"Be reasonable, Dick," said Bill, "I've got five years more experience than you. I eat punks like you for breakfast. Speaking of which, I'm getting hungry."

Dick grinned savagely.

When Bill made another attempt to push past, Dick grabbed him and wrestled him to the ground. He tried to take Bill's rug away, but Bill had a firm hold on it, tucking it under himself to secure it. Dick leapt up and grabbed his own rug.

Bill got up and moved toward the door, but Dick was already there, holding his rolled-up rug aggressively. Bill twisted his mouth and readied his own rug—he was prepared to meet the challenge.

Bill hoisted his rug and charged.

Dick deftly blocked Bill's swing, shoved him back a step, and swung low. Bill parried and countered with a jab at Dick's head. Dick was knocked backward and hit his head on the door of the shoppe. He quickly pulled himself together—he was even more determined now.

The two combatants struggled valiantly in a graceless ballet of flashing red rugs and tan uniforms. One man, then the other, would strike with his rug. Some blows were blocked, while others hit their marks. But neither man was on the verge of surrender.

Time went by slowly, as it does in such situations. Every move, every swing of the rug, was so important to them that the outside world was only a blur.

Then, suddenly, it was all over—Bill was on his knees, unable to continue the fight. His rug slipped from his grasp.

"Hah!" said Dick. "Guess the kid was better than you thought." He picked up Bill's rug and threw it into the parking lot.

"*Ding*," chimed the bell as Dick opened the door to the gift shoppe.

The woman behind the counter stared at him in complete bewilderment. He quickly looked himself over and saw he was a bit worn.

"And how are you this morning?" he said, flirtatiously.

With two fluid movements, Dick swept up the small red rug that lay at the door and put the new red rug in its place. He quickly rolled up the old rug and put it under his arm.

"I'm fine," responded the woman simply, handing him a twenty-dollar bill.

Dick placed the money in his pouch. "Well, have a good day," he said. "See you in four weeks."

"Who will be here in two weeks?" asked the woman slowly.

"Bill should be here. It's his day. Bye."

"Bye."

"*Ding*," the bell chimed once more.

"You'll be here in two weeks, right?" said Dick, as he passed by Bill, who was struggling to his feet.

"Yeah," said Bill, nodding slowly.

"Good," said Dick, tossing the old rug in his truck. He drove away victorious, sweat beading on his brow.

The Adventures of
Merni and Ilk

"I am a friend to all mammals," proclaimed the bearded man standing on the rock that overhung the sea. "And to prove just how incredibly cool I am, I shall jump off of this cliff."

"Uh," began Merni, "I don't think that will prove anything."

"Shut up, Merni," said Ilk. "Let him jump. I've got dibs on his robe."

"What?" said Merni, shocked by his friend's statement. "That's awfully cold."

"Yes, it is cold out here. That's why I want his robe. Hey! Give me your robe. No sense in getting it wet."

The bearded man shook his head.

"Ah, come on," pleaded Ilk. "You're not going to need it anymore."

"Uh," said the bearded man, "I guess you're right. Here you go." He began to remove his robe.

Ilk reached out, but instead of the robe, he seized the bearded man's arm. The bearded man recoiled and they both fell from the cliff. Merni jumped to the edge, grabbing the end of the robe just before it went over.

The robe snapped taut, and he planted his heels deep in the ground to hold the weight.

"Pull me up!" shouted Ilk.

Merni was relieved to hear his friend's voice, but struggled to hold on. He grunted, putting all his effort into the task. In a few seconds, Ilk was back on the cliff.

"Whew," said Ilk. "Thanks."

"Why the hell did you grab him?! He nearly killed you."

"Yeah, something like that."

"What were you thinking?"

"Hey, I wanted his watch too."

"Sheesh. Hey, what are you smiling about?"

Ilk held up the shiny silver watch. "I got it."

Merni just shook his head with a faint grin.

True Love

"Class," said Mrs. Maryweather, "today we will be learning about numbers. And we're going to use our finger paints to draw them."

Johnny wasn't really paying attention—at least, not to his teacher. His bright blue eyes were focused on little Rosey, who happened to be eating her finger paints, and was the most beautiful creature he had ever seen.

She was sitting three chairs over and one up. Her curly dark hair seemed shiny in the fluorescent lights. She was wearing a hideous off-white dress, which didn't complement her light brown skin in the slightest. Not that Johnny really noticed. Being a strapping young lad of six and a half, he just wasn't into that sort of thing. His tastes in clothes extended only to what he or his dad was wearing. And he looked quite nice, he thought, in his red-and-white striped shirt and jeans.

"Johnny," said Mrs. Maryweather calmly, "will you paint me the number seven?"

Johnny thought for a minute. He was pretty sure he learned this one in kindergarten. He dipped his finger into the red paint and then placed it on the paper before him. In only seconds, he had produced a figure that looked remarkably like a seven. He held it up for his teacher to see.

"Very good," she said.

Johnny smiled. He pushed back some of his short, dark-blond hair, not realizing he had used the finger he'd been painting with.

"Oh my word," said Mrs. Maryweather, taking a tissue from the desk and heading straight for the red streak in his hair.

Some of the children chuckled—and so did Johnny. When it was all over, he looked at Rosey, who smiled broadly, her teeth green with paint.

Flarn

Just because someone tells you something doesn't make that something true. In fact, it's likely bullshit. Very likely. And that's just what Flarn Cornsnipple, of Zarnarax 7, was finding out.

Flarn was listening to a man tell him about the ancient city of silver-plated golden artifacts of the long extinct civilization of Globulosious. It was a subject Flarn was very knowledgeable on already, and he couldn't fathom what he was hearing from the fellow. How could one man get so much so wrong and still believe every word of it? Flarn wondered.

It wasn't just that the fellow was an idiot. He was a highly educated idiot. That is to say, he had spent enough time in enough schools that he should have actually learned something useful. At least, that's what he had indicated to Flarn.

Still, Flarn Cornsnipple, of Zarnarax 7, listened politely, as was his way. Later, of course, he would probably want to smack the man. But for now, at least, he would just tolerate it all. He did, after all, have better things to do.

Flarn's mind drifted to the task that lay before him. It was going to be difficult, but strangely relaxing. He decided not to reason out how it could be both, and just go with the flow.

Soon the guy was talking about the Straits of Hoospooton like he knew what that bit was all about. Flarn was having a hard time listening to this now. This was just stupid.

"Uh," said Flarn, "you don't have to cross the Hoospooton Straits. It's a metaphorical concept. The straits are in your mind. You have to use the Boat of Consuigo de Rootuin. Which, strangely, is a real boat. You sit in it and row, both with your hands and with your mind."

The man stared at Flarn for a second. "I've studied the manuscripts," the man said. "You have to cross the straits to get to the other side and begin your journey up the Hill of Tomath. I studied ancient civilizations in college—"

"You obviously were not paying attention in class," said Flarn Cornsnipple, abruptly. "The Hill of Tomath actually refers to a whorehouse where the journey of the First Seekers of Truth stopped after successfully using the Boat. They said they didn't know it was a whorehouse when they stopped, which is kind of odd, since the video recordings of the journey clearly indicate a large sign in front of the place declaring it to be a whorehouse.

"You see, I've been on follow-up expeditions. And I can tell you, you've obviously watched way too much entertainment programming on the video-net. It's true that, in an old program, the Hoospooton Straits were actual straits. It's become a fairly common misconception in the real world, thanks to countless reruns. I wouldn't feel too bad about getting it all mixed up. Well, I've got to run. Enjoy your day."

Flarn hurried out of the shop while he was still on top. He didn't want to get into any pointless arguments. He was on a mission—an important one. The retrieval of the Seven Scepters of King Scoriposis was now foremost on his mind.

The Case of the
Perplexing Enigma

The doorbell rang.

Zebow Butron almost jumped out of his pale blue-gray skin. He had been resting in his chair with his feet up on his desk, gazing aimlessly out the second-story window of his office. The view wasn't that spectacular, not compared to some of the places he'd been. Not the least of which was his homeworld of Googalgon-7. But since he had set up his office in this building, he found himself often staring out at the clouds and whatever else happened to float or fly by.

This time he must have dozed off a little, for he remembered dreaming about a small dog and going for a long walk with a pretty, young Earth girl named Susie. He didn't know any girls named Susie, so it must have been a dream. In fact, the only Earth girl he knew was named Chantel, and, while she enjoyed going for long walks with him, she was just a friend.

Zebow straightened his desk and said, "Come in."

The door didn't open.

"Uh," said Zebow, raising his voice, "come in."

Still, the door didn't open.

He got up and went over to the door and opened it. There was no one in the hall, but on the floor lay a brown cardboard box about five inches long by three inches wide and three inches deep. He looked at it carefully. Nowhere on its visible surface was there any indication as to what it contained or to whom it was for. He went back to his desk and retrieved his scanner.

As he ran the device over the box, he scrutinized the display. *Nothing dangerous*, he thought to himself. The contents, however, remained a mystery, as the scanner showed nothing. He slipped the device into his shirt pocket, then picked up the box and took it to his desk, closing the door behind him.

★ ★ ★

It was another typical day in the offices of Zebow Butron, Alien Detective. Zebow sat around, stared out the window, and occasionally got up to pet his Flectonian fish. It was a quiet day.

The doorbell rang.

This was odd, as the doorbell had been broken for months. Zebow just about jumped out of his purplish skin. He quickly collected the bits of himself that had managed to escape.

The master sleuth reasoned that the doorbell must have corrected itself, and that there must be someone at the door.

"Come in," he said.

No one entered.

He opened the door himself, fully expecting someone to be waiting. There was no one outside. He shrugged—at least, the parts that were good at shrugging—and went back inside.

The Flectonian fish was resting peacefully on the sofa, its lightly whiskered head falling lazily off the edge.

"Now that was strange, Milton," said Zebow. "That doorbell hasn't worked for months, and when it finally does, there's no one there."

The fish flapped its hind flipper.

Zebow sat at his desk and stared out the window.

The doorbell rang again.

"Hmmm," said Zebow, "come in?"

Nobody responded.

The detective thought for a moment, then got up and opened the door. As before, there was no one there. He looked up and down the street, but there was nothing suspicious. He went back inside, then popped his head out again. Still nothing suspicious.

He pressed the doorbell button; nothing happened.

He pressed it again to be sure. Still nothing.

Zebow stepped inside and shut the door. He took two steps—then the doorbell rang again. He quickly spun around and opened the door. There was nothing there. He went to his desk and got his tools.

The doorbell button came off easily, and it checked out fine. He stood on a chair and opened the doorbell itself. Everything seemed to be in working order. He made the doorbell ring a couple of times, then put it back together.

He reached outside and pressed the button.

Nothing happened.

His face flowed through a rainbow of bright colors.

Zebow went to the sofa and petted his fish.

He thought for a moment, then half expected the doorbell to ring. The door was open, and he looked out on the street. He jumped up and closed the door.

Now he waited.

He stood by the door. And he waited.

He walked around the room. And he waited.

He petted his fish some more. And—the doorbell rang.

Zebow scrunched up his face. Then he opened a drawer and pulled out a small device. The rectangular item contained a display and was encrusted with lights and buttons.

As he ran the thing over the wall, lights flashed, beeps sounded, and a continuous readout swirled around the screen. He scanned around the doorbell button, and around the door and the doorbell itself.

"Ah," said Zebow Butron, examining the display. "It was so obvious, Milton."

The Flectonian fish flapped its flipper.

"There is a time warp in the wall," continued Zebow. "Just between the button and the doorbell. As best I can tell, it's causing a four-month delay between the pushing of the button and the sounding of the bell. Hmmmm. How annoying."

The fish had drifted back to sleep.

Zebow rummaged through some of his things, then got out his tools.

He spread some old junk out on the floor and began fitting things together. A few hours later, he stood up holding a haphazardly constructed device.

"Hope for the best, Milton," he said, placing the strange device on the wall. It attached itself immediately, and Zebow pressed a button before diving for the sofa.

The device hummed, then screeched, then hummed again, then, finally, popped and fell off the wall.

Zebow moved his scanner over the wall. He reached outside and pressed the button; the doorbell rang. He walked over and petted his fish.

"I guess my homemade *Temporal Inversion Thrust Compensator* worked," he said. The fish rolled over to get its belly petted.

"How about I get you some dinner?"

The Flectonian fish perked up.

"Yes, that's just what I'll do."

Time Out

"It's five o'clock, Jim," said Bob. "Time to go home."

Jim sat in his chair, staring out of the second-story window.

"Hey," said Bob, grabbing Jim's shoulder and causing him to jump, "let's go."

Jim looked up at Bob. "Go where?" he said.

"Where do you think? Home, of course. That is, if you still want a ride."

Jim looked down at his watch—it read 3:02. "Is it five already? My watch must need a new battery."

"You've been staring out that window too long. Let's go."

They went down to the car together.

At home, Jim sat down for a bite. He looked at the clock on the wall—2:15. *Was every clock of his broken?* His watch, with a new battery in place, agreed with the clock. He was sure he had set his watch to the correct time.

He turned on the television. Ah—there was the time. He set his watch to 7:04 p.m.

"It can't be that late," he said.

He adjusted the clock in the kitchen as well, then looked at his watch to confirm the time—1:20 p.m.

"What the hell is going on?"

He felt like he needed a nap.

He woke up and looked at his digital alarm clock.

12:00 a.m.

"No way is it that late," he said.

He got up, paced a bit, went to the bathroom, then went back to bed. He looked at the clock again.

12:00 a.m.

"Shit."

He went back to sleep.

When he woke again, the clock was blinking, flashing 12:00 a.m. over and over.

Jim picked it up and shook it. It was obviously morning—the light through the windows made that clear.

12:00 a.m.

"What's wrong with this thing?"

12:00 a.m.

He checked his watch.

12:00 a.m.

He ran to the kitchen.

12:00 a.m.

He went back to the bedroom.

12:00 a.m.

12:00 a.m.

12:00 a.m.

"This is weird."

12:0—

He blinked out of existence.

Eating Ice Cream

Being nice. Being kind. Being good. She had had enough.

Now she would kill. Kill. Kill.

And eat ice cream.

Plain vanilla ice cream.

Ice cream was good. She liked ice cream. She liked to lick an ice-cream cone up one side and down the other. This drove the boys crazy. The ice cream would slowly melt and run vanilla streaks down the cone, over her hand, and drip to the floor. She liked driving the boys crazy.

Lick. Lick. Lick.

Drip. Drip. Drip.

Kill. Kill. Kill.

How Can You Not See That

"I see Nazis everywhere. They are in the streets, under my bed, in my soup. Everywhere. Why is the world being overrun by Nazis?"

The psychiatrist leaned back comfortably in his chair. He made a few notes in the spiral-bound notepad in his hand. "Perhaps you only *believe* you see Nazis because you've been conditioned to see them," he said, calmly. "Do you watch a lot of television? Or perhaps scroll through the internet or social media posts, actively looking for images of Nazis, to reinforce your beliefs?"

"What? No, they are everywhere. I'm not crazy."

"Well, you came to see me, so you are obviously in search of an affirmation that what you are seeing is—or isn't—real. So there must be some doubt, no?"

"Yes, I suppose. I mean, some of the places I see Nazis obviously can't be real—it just doesn't make sense. Yet, I see them, clear as day. So my real question is: how are they showing up in all of these places? What is their goal? How can they be stopped?"

The psychiatrist made a few more notes. "If you were living in Nazi Germany, this would make a little more sense. But that was around ninety years ago. So, would you agree that Nazis no longer exist?"

"No, I most certainly would *not* agree! I see them everywhere, they are in the government, the grocery stores, my neighbor's shed. I know they are up to something. *How can you not see that?*"

"You just said 'Nazi.'"

"What?"

"Nothing." The psychiatrist adjusted himself in his chair. "I have a theory—you may be suffering from delusions and hallucinations. Possibly due to cult programming, or too many illicit drugs. I'm going to prescribe some medication that should sort you out.

There was a knock on the door.

"Yes?" said the psychiatrist.

The door opened slightly. The receptionist poked her head in and motioned for the psychiatrist.

"One moment," said the psychiatrist, as he got up and walked to the door. He stood there for a moment. The door opened just enough to reveal a man dressed in an old French military uniform: a gray coat adorned with medals and golden epaulets, with a large two-pointed hat.

"*Heil* . . ." said the psychiatrist, too softly to be heard clearly, before closing the door and returning to his chair.

"Sorry about that," said the psychiatrist.

"I just saw Napoleon! They're all coming—to take over the world, destroy our freedom to mutilate ourselves and our children, to have abortions so we don't need to take responsibility for our actions, and make cheap foreign goods inaccessible to people with no money. Down with the rich!"

"Oh, that was just Doug," said the psychiatrist. "He tries to conquer the offices every few weeks. He's harmless."

"You're part of it! You're a racist! *I* am the righteous!"

The psychiatrist sighed. "Everything will be all right. Here's that prescription. I will have it sent to the pharmacy downstairs."

The patient farted.

"Now doesn't that feel better?" asked the psychiatrist.

"I can't talk to you ever again," said the patient, getting up and running to the door. "Goodbye!"

The Toilet

I went to the bathroom,
    And what did I see
A bright, shiny toilet
    Staring right back at me
I looked to the left,
    And then to the right,
I lifted the lid
    To see what was inside

Eyeing its contents,
    And not wanting a scandal
I closed it up tight,
    And jiggled the handle

I waited and jiggled
    Then sighed with a hush
I jiggled again,
    But there was no flush

I turned to the tank,

And there I scowled
The ballcock assembly
    Must have been fouled
The chain may have broken
    Not pulling, and thus
Not raising the flapper—
    Causing said flush

Peering inside,
    I was surprised there to see
It was missing the parts
    There expected to be
What kind of technology
    To have made such a thing
There was little inside
    Except a wee bit of string

What wizardry, a marvel
    What style, what grace
I slipped on the floor
    And fell flat on my face
Climbing to my feet,
    Regaining composure,
I looked back in the tank
    And resumed my disclosure

A string from the handle
    Went down to a knob
And went on to a cork
    Which floated and bobbed
Through the murky blue liquid

I could barely make out
Electrical streaks
    Darting about

It was clear to me now
    This was no simple chore
I pulled myself up
    And walked to the door
Help was needed,
    In this delicate matter
For soon it would be
    Time to empty my bladder

I rang up a plumber
    And what should appear
But a middle-aged fat man
    Smelling of beer
As he bent over the stool
    About to begin
His mighty butt crack
    About did me in

He coughed as he leaned
    And groaned as he stood
"This tank wasn't cleaned,
    This fluid is no good."

"How much to repair?"
    Inquired my spouse.
"How much to repair
    And get out of my house?!"

He pulled out some tea
    From the back of his truck
He said it was free
    Plus five hundred bucks

Thog, Caveman Visionary

"Ugh," said Thog. "How go search for mate?"

"Ar," said Togath, lowering his head, "not go so well. Thog help?"

The two friends walked along, dragging their clubs, as was the style of the day. They were clad in the smelliest, grimiest of skins—very fashionable. It took a lot of bloody carcass-beating and not bathing to achieve the desired effect. Still, it hadn't been enough to win Togath a mate.

"Ugh, Togath should club big beast to impress woman. It work for Thog."

"Ar, I give it try."

"Ugh, Thog wait by stream."

"Ar."

Thog continued on to the stream as Togath went off into the woods to find a big beast to club. Thog sat on the bank and watched the clear water flow by, then dipped his hand in and let the water go smoothly through his fingers. He splashed some on his face. He often wondered where the water came from. He knew it came from the sky, of course; but the hows and whys eluded him. So many things seemed to come from the sky: wind, lightning, rain, as well as other things. He scooped up some water and had a drink.

Looking up, he saw Morgoth standing on the other side of the stream, spear in hand.

"Ugh, Morgoth spear many fish."

"Ga," said Morgoth.

Morgoth did indeed spear many fish, reflected Thog. He was one of the premier fishermen of the tribe. "Ugh," said Thog, grinning.

Thog went back to dreaming about the water. Then he saw something shining in the stream. It appeared to be a streak of light dancing on the surface. He quickly realized it was the reflection of something. He thought it might be the sun, but the sun's reflection was far away from this streak. Then he looked up and saw it—a streak of light hurtling toward the ground.

"Ugh, Morgoth duck!"

"Ga, Morgoth not duck. Morgoth man."

"Ugh," said Thog, jumping up and pointing frantically.

"Ga?" said Morgoth, watching Thog's display. He looked up just as the streak of light hit him square in the head.

Thog threw his head back in surprise as both Morgoth and the light fell to the ground. A gentle *whump* seemed to follow the event, fading into the peaceful calm of the stream.

Thog crossed the stream to help him. Morgoth's spear was lying on the ground, alongside Morgoth, who lay motionless, but still breathing.

Thog could find no evidence of the light that had struck Morgoth. But he did notice a strange-looking, fist-sized rock near Morgoth's feet. The rock was blackened, pitted, quite heavy, and a bit warm. He put it in his pouch for later examination.

But what had happened to the light? He couldn't quite get his mind around it. The light had clearly struck Morgoth with some force. And what of this rock that seemed to be where the light had fallen? Had it been uncovered by the light hitting the ground? He just didn't have any answers.

Perhaps the light had been a fireball. There were tales of the fireballs which occasionally streaked through the sky actually striking the ground—sometimes with grave consequences. That must be it. Morgoth was struck by a fireball. The fireball then hit the ground where the rock was, blackening and pitting the rock. It was all starting to make sense.

But what of the fireball? Where did it go? Perhaps it entered the rock. That would certainly cause the rock to become warm. The rock *was* blackened as if it had been in a fire. Now he was getting somewhere.

Thog looked up at the sky. Were there more fireballs up there waiting to rain down upon him or someone else? Where, exactly, did they come from? Yet another thing that came from the sky with little or no warning and absolutely no explanation.

"Ugh," he said in frustration.

So many things in the world raised so many questions for Thog. And there were few answers. The explanations given by the shamans didn't always work for him, though he recognized their wisdom. But he often saw things in ways they didn't.

He looked up at the sky again. At night there were many points of light in the sky. Perhaps they were the source of the fireballs. But if that were true, he and everyone else were in extreme danger, as there were many more points of light than he could count. But if the lights were not fireballs, then what were they?

"Pa," said Nokoth, standing on the other side of the stream, "what happened Morgoth?"

"Ugh," said Thog, sadly, "Morgoth hit by fireball from sky." He pointed to the sky, then to Morgoth.

"*Pa*," said Nokoth incredulously. He made his way across the stream and joined Thog.

Thog knew there was no point in explaining his theories to Nokoth. Nokoth wouldn't understand, and didn't care anyway. Nokoth only cared about one thing—spearing fish.

"Pa," said Nokoth, examining the scene, "this spear of Morgoth. Morgoth dead. Nokoth now spear more fish." Nokoth picked up Morgoth's spear.

"Ugh," said Thog, making his way back across the stream. He sat down on the bank, retrieving the rock from his pouch. Had the fireball really entered it? And why was it no longer warm? He looked into the sky for answers, knowing full well there were none to be found. The sky was blue and almost cloudless—just wisps of white here and there.

"Pa!" said Nokoth, waving his new spear which now had a fish stuck on the end of it.

Morgoth began to stir. "Ga! What happened Morgoth?" he said as he got to his feet.

"Ugh, Morgoth not duck," said Thog, looking up briefly before returning to his thoughts. He would discuss what had happened with his friend Togath—he would listen and not think Thog a fool. He looked up again to see Morgoth tackling Nokoth, and taking back his spear.

He heard someone coming—Togath. His skins were badly torn, and he was bloody from head to toe. He was dragging his club lower than was usual.

"Ugh," said Thog, "Togath club big beast?"

"Arrrr," said Togath, shaking his head slowly, "I try again later."

"Ugh."

Togath joined his friend on the bank for a cool drink of water, and they shared their stories.

Of Astronauts and Lettuce

Commander Shelby was flying along in his spaceship one day thinking about lettuce, as he often did. He thought about a particularly green, leafy head of lettuce. He would think of different ways to prepare it for a meal. He would think of ways he could use it for astronaut stuff, like flapping the leaves fast enough to fly.

It was on this day, however, he was thinking about just what lettuce was all about, in a cosmic sense that is. And he was determined to find out, even if he had to search the galaxy for someone wise and old and, preferably, just plain up on lettuce.

Shelby zoomed over to the planet Connie, a neat place—never dirty—where travelers often stopped to ask directions. At the local super-ultra-high octane rocket fuel service station, he talked at length with the man behind the Megacred counter.

"Can you point me," said Shelby, "in the general direction of some wise and old and, preferably, just plain up on lettuce person?"

"Well," said the Megacred man, thinking for a moment. "I suggest you travel five light-years due north. That's galactic north, you understand, not planetary north, but then I imagine you knew that, didn't you?"

Shelby nodded that he did.

"Good," said the clerk. He continued: "Make a left at the lime gelatin, and follow the trail of peanut brittle to the—"

"Er," said Shelby, raising his hand to interrupt. "What's that bit about lime gelatin?"

"Oh, take a right at the lime gelatin and—"

"Er, no. I mean . . . What's lime gelatin doing in space?"

"Not much, really. It seems to enjoy itself, so no one bothers it."

"Oh. Go ahead."

"Anyway, after the peanut brittle, you should come to the planet Nameless Orb. It seems no one cared to name it, doesn't matter much either way, nothing but talking fish and some kind of hyperintelligent plant life or some such, not very interesting. Uh . . . where was I?"

"Nameless Orb," said Shelby, taking notes.

"Ah, yes," continued the clerk. "Just make a right and there you are. Well, you'll have to travel a few hundred light-years, but you can't miss it."

"Er, got it."

With that, Commander Shelby was off. That is to say, he was off to seek out the wise old prophet of which the Megacred man had spoken.

He headed five light-years due north, galactic north, made a left at the lime gelatin, but not without stopping to take a few pictures, and then followed the trail of peanut brittle to a nameless orb. No. It was *the* Nameless Orb. Excitement swelled within him at the realization. Shelby was so close to his goal that he didn't waste time stopping to talk to the fish or interrogate the flora. He made a right, and then, a few hundred light-years later . . .

Commander Shelby landed his spaceship on a planet, and strolled around a large city. He asked a passerby for directions to the person he sought.

He made his way to an apartment complex. He knocked on a door.

"Yes?" said an old, frail voice from inside.

"I am seeking an old sage," said Shelby. "Someone who can tell me all I need to know about lettuce."

"Oh," said the voice, "come in then."

Shelby entered the dwelling. Inside sat an old man in a worn-out recliner, holding a battered flyswatter. The man gestured with the swatter for Shelby to come in.

"So," said the old man, "you want to know about lettuce, do you, sonny?"

"Yes," answered Shelby. "I have come a great distance to find someone who can tell me just what lettuce is all about—in a cosmic sense. Can you help?"

"Well, I reckon I can, sonny."

The old man gathered himself, then abruptly swatted a fly.

"Lettuce," he began, "is first and foremost—green."

Shelby nodded excitedly.

"Settle down now, I ain't got to the good part yet."

The old man paused.

"It's also floppy," he said finally.

He swatted another fly.

"Are you still with me?"

Shelby nodded again.

"Good," said the old sage. "Now, when you combine these two elements—the greenness and the floppiness—well, now you really got something. You can do all kinds of things. Like up in a spaceship, you can flap it, and fly around. Yeah, that's a good one. Now, I think it's great on sandwiches, myself. A little lettuce, some tomato, some mayonnaise, and whatever meat you like. Now you're talkin' good eatin'."

"But," said Shelby, "what of its cosmic significance?"

"Its *what?*"

"The reason I sought you out. Lettuce's cosmic place in the universe."

"Oh, that. Well, between two slices of wheat bread is generally where I put it. Cosmically or otherwise. It's lettuce! Now beat it!"

Shelby left as the old sage brandished his flyswatter menacingly, swatting the air in Shelby's direction for good measure.

On the flight home, Commander Shelby thought about what the wise old sage had told him about lettuce. It all made perfect sense. It was all so simple. And now, it was time for a sandwich. He gathered lettuce, tomatoes, mayonnaise, and some sliced meat from the storage unit. He placed it all between two slices of wheat bread, just as the old sage had suggested. He took a bite. He enjoyed it.

He now felt he understood, truly understood, the cosmic place of lettuce. It was *inside him* all along. It was in his stomach.

The Electricity Wells
of Grabnar-3

"Go and fetch me a bucket of E-lectricity, boy," said the old man from his rocking chair.

"But Pa, it's a-rainin'," said the youth sitting on the floor.

"Now don't you go a-backtalkin' me. Jus' slip on yer suit and git out thar."

"Ah heck," said the youth, getting to his feet. He went to the closet and pulled out the dingy rain suit.

Outside it was pouring. Bucket in hand, the young man threw the hood over his head and stepped off the porch. The forty-watt raindrops crackled as they spattered against the fine metallic mesh of the rain suit. He headed toward the well.

At the well, the youth lowered the well bucket and let it fill for a minute. Then he raised it. He poured the liquid electricity into his own bucket and started back toward the run-down shack they called a house.

He suddenly realized that he had bigger ambitions. This was not the place he wanted to live. It wasn't where he wanted to be. *It wasn't—*

Thunder boomed, shattering his train of thought.

He hurried back to the house—a strike was imminent.

Just as he reached the porch, a drenching flood of water fell from the sky. He dove for the door—and made it.

"Didn't spill a drop, boy," said the old man. "Nice work."

The young man removed his rain suit and headed off to bed. He dreamed all night of leaving the place—except in one dream, where he was married to a supermodel.

The Abduction of Harry

Harry Crantz was walking along the path that led through the woods behind his house in North Carolina. It was well after noon, though he wasn't really sure of the exact time. He was lost in the moment: the smell of pine sap and old beer cans, the sight of squirrels darting about. The air was cool for the summer, but not unseasonably so. He stopped to kick a dead squirrel out of the path.

There had been a lot of dead squirrels turning up recently. Not many people had noticed, except Harry. He often noticed things that others missed. Like how the local CD store would open CDs, play them, throw them around or whatever, and then seal them back up and sell them as new. He also noticed strange flashing lights in the night sky. He didn't tell anyone about that though.

Harry had just turned thirty-five last Saturday. It had been a rather uneventful day. He met a woman, then met another woman, decided that he loved both of them, and asked out a third woman instead. She, of course, had said, "No thank you." It often worked like this for him.

He turned up the path toward the street and found himself already down by the convenience store. The suddenness surprised him. He stopped and bought a newspaper.

Harry walked on to the park and had a seat on a bench. It was his usual routine this time of year. He skimmed through the paper: *Two eight-year-olds arrested in school for pointing their fingers in a socially dangerous manner; claims of nose picking went unheard.* "What's the world coming to," he mumbled to himself.

The article wasn't very clear. The local paper was clearly run by imbeciles, its editor having peaked in third grade and decided that was high enough. Still, the misspellings and bizarre similes were amusing.

Thump!

Harry turned his head. Lying on the grass behind his bench was a squirrel. A dead squirrel.

Now that was new. He looked up. It must have fallen from a tree. Except—there was no tree. In fact, there was nothing overhead but open sky.

He got up and went around to look at the dead squirrel. It hadn't been shot. In fact, there wasn't a mark on it. He looked around, scanning the area. He wondered where it could have come from. Perhaps it jumped. From where, though—the nearest tree was a hundred feet away. It was odd. He was getting hungry. He would have to eat something before he could think about this further.

Harry rolled up his paper and headed home.

When he arrived at his house he went to the kitchen and began fixing himself a sandwich. He had just opened the mustard jar when the phone rang.

"Hello," he said.

"Hi," said the woman's voice on the phone. "May I speak with Harry Crantz?"

"That's me."

"Hello, how are you doing? My name is Tiffany, I'm calling people in your area to let them—"

He hung up.

He spread the mustard on a slice of bread. Then he found some lettuce in the back of the refrigerator. He tore off the brown bits until something resembling green appeared. The phone rang again.

"Hello?" he said.

"Mr. Crintz?"

"No, but if you find him, tell him I'm tired of his calls." He hung up.

The phone rang again.

"Yes?"

"Mr. Crantz," said a man's voice, "how would you like to be rich beyond your wildest dreams?"

"Sounds good," said Harry.

"We're holding a free seminar—"

"No thanks." He hung up.

Harry tossed the lettuce on his sandwich, added some meat, and decided that was close enough to food. The phone rang again.

"Yes," he said wearily—this was one more annoying call than usual.

"Is this Harry Crantz?" The voice was gruff and determined.

"Yes."

"My name is not important. But I know that you know that something strange has been happening to the local squirrel population."

"And how do you know that?"

"That's not important either. But if you want to know more, meet me at your favorite park bench tomorrow at noon."

"Why not meet tonight? It's not that late."

"I'm sorry, but I have two other appointments with people who know things that you don't know, but I know they know, and they need to know what I know more than you need to know."

"I see." He didn't really.

"So, you'll be there?"

"Yes, I'll be there."

"One more thing."

"Yes?"

"If a man calls wanting to sell you siding—"

"Yes?"

"Hang up. It's not nearly as good a deal as it sounds."

"Thanks for the tip."

The phone clicked. Harry hung up.

He ate his sandwich.

At noon the next day, Harry Crantz waited on his favorite park bench for the owner of the gruff voice to appear. He hoped it wouldn't take long—he was already hungry again.

You Want It, We'll Get It

Captain John Wilham stood on the edge of the largest canyon on planet 445-X-4. He looked down at the reddish ground at the bottom. Patches of brown grass-like stuff moved slowly around, presumably doing whatever it is moving grass does. The jagged walls looked challenging, but what he was after was at the bottom. Little things like moving grass and jagged walls weren't going to deter him. He and his two crewmates were in the retrieval business. In this case, it happened they were after a Farnooshian Blue Bush. A small, fern sort of thing said to promote good health and sexual prowess. Most of the stranger and harder to come by plants in the universe were said to do this, but as long as he was paid well he wasn't going to argue. Why it was called a Farnooshian Blue Bush was completely unclear, as it was not found anywhere near Farnooshia, and it wasn't at all blue. Beige. It was definitely beige. Still, there was no disputing its value.

He climbed down the jagged wall of the canyon. It was slow going, but soon he was on the bottom. He gingerly stepped around the quietly moving grass, being very careful not to get too close to it.

According to the information the client had provided, the Farnooshian Blue Bush was to be found in a small cave just ahead of his current position. The directions were from an ancient text, and likely to be somewhat inaccurate.

Captain Wilham moved past a large rock and saw a cave.

Of course, sometimes those texts were very accurate.

He switched on his flashlight and went inside. He walked a few yards, turned left, then right. Then he saw it—and another, and another.

In a roundish cave about ten yards across, there were more Farnooshian Blue Bushes than he could count. He checked the contract. One bush. That's all he needed; that's all he would get. The bushes were small—a foot tall and half as wide—and very beige.

He grabbed one and pulled. It resisted his efforts. He pulled harder and out of the ground it came. He beat some of the dirt off the roots and stuffed the plant into his pack.

He switched off his flashlight as he exited the cave. He headed back to the section of wall where he had climbed down. As he started to walk past the brown patches of grass-like stuff he noticed they weren't moving. This was clearly a bad sign. He quickened his pace.

The brown patches suddenly moved to block his path. Then they began growing, each blade of grass becoming an increasingly long tentacle.

Captain Wilham leapt over the grass and rolled. More grass approached. He jumped to the rocks as brown tentacles reached for him. Up the rock wall he went.

At the top, he dusted himself off and glanced over the edge. Apparently, the stuff couldn't climb.

The single yellow sun was setting to the west as he made his way back to his ship, the oddly named Sniffwhistle. When asked why he named his ship Sniffwhistle, he always refused to explain, hinting only that it involved a lost bet.

"Have a nice sightseeing, John?" asked Tilman as Captain Wilham walked up the cargo ramp. Tilman was tall, thin, and fair haired. He was jovial and generally fun to be around.

"It was very impressive," said Captain Wilham, his voice resonating with authority. "Secure the ship." He placed the Farnooshian Blue Bush into the hold in a secure container.

Tilman sealed the outer door and cleared the airlock area of anything that might have come aboard uninvited.

Captain John Wilham made his way to the bridge.

"Let's get out of here," said Captain Wilham, taking a seat next to the pilot.

"I thought it was a nice place," said Liddia, adjusting the controls and igniting the engines.

Captain Wilham took some readings from the screens, and then stared out at the terrain. He panned the cameras, checking all around the ship.

"Everything reads secure," said Liddia.

The captain didn't say anything.

"Okay," said Liddia. "Off we go."

Once the ship had cleared the atmosphere and was headed for open space, Liddia made another attempt with the captain, who was still quietly staring at the screens. "You're not going to go nuts and jump out an airlock, are you?" she said, smiling.

"No," said the captain.

"So, what's up?"

"What do you mean?"

"Can't you tell? You're a little distant."

"Yes, I suppose. Don't worry, I wasn't bitten by anything. I think."

"I wasn't worried. Not much, anyway. I guess you were just awestruck by the magnificence of the place. Right?" She grinned. She had a powerful face, attractive but strong, framed by long black hair. When she smiled, it often seemed to indicate that she didn't intend to kill you, at least not anytime soon.

"Actually, I was thinking about what was going to be done with this acquisition. It's none of my business, I know. But—it seems a shame to just hand it over to these bastards. Let's start up a new business."

"Like what?"

"Like space monkey smuggling."

"Hah!" Liddia almost fell out of her seat. "You must be kidding. You know how much trouble space monkeys are."

"Yeah, I know. Oh well."

Tilman burst into the room. "Hey! We're under attack! Pirates! Look!" he said, pointing out the window.

Captain Wilham and Liddia looked out the window at three rather large whitish ships that were now approaching. The sunlight glinted off of their hulls as they drew nearer.

"Pirates wouldn't approach so we could see them," said the captain. "And those ships are much too big to be pirates. They must be corporate executives."

"I don't think they intend to stop," said Liddia. "I'm evading."

"Hey," said the captain, as Liddia steered the ship. "Why didn't the proximity alarms go off?" As he finished speaking, every alarm in the ship seemed to go off, and things started shaking—little things, like the walls, floor, and coffeemaker.

"I saw them when I was looking out a window below," said Tilman, trying to be helpful.

"These ships are so big," said Liddia, her voice trembling excitedly, "that they appear to have their own gravitational influence. Apparently, they'd just come into the detector's range."

"They are big," said the captain.

The ships were indeed big, now nearly filling up the screens that showed views from many angles around the ship.

Once they had filled up the screens, the shaking stopped as the internal gravity compensators adjusted themselves.

An eerie silence fell over the crew. They peered up and around at the large vessels. Whitish ships were virtually all they could see, lit by the light from each ship.

"Hello there," said a voice over the comm-system, startling everyone on the bridge. "Hello, anyone at home?"

"Uh . . ." started the captain, "yes?"

"I don't mean to interrupt your affairs," said the voice, "but I am in need of your services. If you wouldn't mind joining me aboard my ship—"

"Who, exactly, are you?" asked the captain, politely.

"Oh, I'm just a fellow in need of some assistance in a delicate matter. I'll just have someone guide you folks over here. Then we can have a nice chat, and some juice."

Directions were being relayed to the nav-computer, and the little light lit up asking if it would be all right to let the computer guide them in. Liddia hated that little light. It was a pretentious thing. But it made situations like this quite a lot easier.

She looked at the captain, who was looking at the little light. He gestured, and she pressed the appropriate button. The little light that lit up indicating that the ship was now in the control of the computer lit up. And off went the ship.

It slowly made its way down the underbelly of the large vessel above them. Up through a large passage it rose. Down another. Then, quietly it came to rest on a docking platform.

"Well," said the captain, "I guess we get out and see what it's all about."

The captain, Liddia, and Tilman were greeted outside of the ship by a small robotic figure. It gestured for them to follow.

After leaving the docking bay, they went down a long hall, then came to an elevator. Shortly they exited the elevator and went down another hall, then another, and then they came to a door. The robot knocked on the door then let them in.

"Ah," said the strange fellow in the swivel chair, "there you are. So good to see you. Please, come in and sit down."

The fellow was purple, and had two more arms than was the norm. He motioned to the robots to fluff up the pillows of the plush sofas that lay huddled around the center of the room then shooed them away.

The crew of Sniffwhistle sauntered in and sat down.

"What gives?" asked Captain Wilham, as directly as possible.

The purple man grinned. "You mean," he said, "why have I abducted you and your crew?"

"Yes," said Captain Wilham, "that is precisely what I mean. This sort of thing doesn't happen everyday, so I hope you have a good reason for this inconvenience to us."

"I appreciate your spirit, you must be the captain, correct? Yes, I thought so, and the rest of your crew?"

"That's Tilman, and this is Liddia. I'm Captain John Wilham. Now, who are you?"

"Oh, no need to be so blunt, I am Zargo Flingo. Perhaps you have heard of me?"

Zargo Flingo was the premier stockholder in the Sotron-Mega Corporation, and was quite possibly the richest being in the known galaxy. A philanthropist, buyer and seller of whole planets, and apparently owner of three unbelievably huge spacecraft: oh yes, they had heard of him.

"*The*," said Tilman completely awestruck, "Zargo Flingo?"

"There could be no other," said Zargo, grinning.

"Okay," said Captain Wilham, "so what does the richest person in the universe want with us?"

"Oh," said Zargo, modestly, "I'm not the richest person in the universe. Not as far as anyone can prove anyway." He grinned again, playing with one of his many rings, which possibly contained a micro-galaxy. "It's simple really," said Zargo, "I need you to fetch something for me. That's all really."

"Why can't you do it?"

"It must be done in the most discreet manner, and as you can see," he waved an arm around the extravagant room, "I am far from discreet."

Captain Wilham looked at his crew who just shrugged. He turned back to his host. "Do we have a choice?" he asked.

"Do you have a choice?" repeated Zargo. "Of course you have a choice. I am not a hostile man, I wouldn't force anyone to do anything. In fact, I intend to pay you quite a handsome sum to perform this all too simple a task. How does that sound?"

"There's more to it than you've said," said Liddia, "isn't there?"

"There's always more to it," responded Zargo, "but it should pose no problem for your crew's remarkable abilities. Nothing of consequence I should think."

"Why don't you let us decide that," said Captain Wilham. "Please, fill us in."

"Very well," said Zargo. "You just have to go to Cantor Prime. Once there, you'll retrieve a small package from a fellow named Forquat. He will meet you in the lobby of the Libantan Hotel, near the spaceport."

"I see," said Captain Wilham, "you want us to go to the hottest party planet in the galaxy, and pick up a thing for you."

"That's right."

"How much do you intend to pay us for this service?"

Zargo Flingo passed a luminescent sheet to Captain Wilham, who glanced at it before passing it on to his crew. The look on their faces indicated that they were all on the same wavelength.

"You have yourself a deal," said Captain Wilham.

★ ★ ★

The Sniffwhistle landed at Starport One—the primary spaceport of the hottest party planet in the galaxy: Cantor Prime. The crew felt the warmth of the sun as they left the ship and walked toward the terminal. They were greeted by scantily clad women from some of the more exotic parts of the universe and given ten free chips, which could be used to buy some simple services and goods such as beverages, snacks, requests for ladies to put their tops back on (a rarely used service, but there had been times), and some other things too unimportant to mention. Captain John Wilham led the way through the terminal, where proper forms had to be signed and out onto the streets of Cantor Prime.

For as far as the eye could see, half naked people frolicked. Some fully naked people frolicked, as well. And there were even those that were completely dressed. If one were to count them all, the fully clothed were actually in the majority, but no one really noticed. Either way, there was much frolicking.

Tilman closely watched the girl bouncing up and down next to him. His eyes never wavered from her body. He could feel something tugging at him, pulling him along.

"Come on," said Liddia, grabbing Tilman's arm with both hands, "quit ogling her, we've got a job to do."

Tilman waved to the young lady as he was dragged away. She smiled and waved back, then the crowd swallowed her up.

"That was just mean," said Tilman.

"You'll get over it," replied Liddia.

"The hotel is a block away," said Captain Wilham. "I estimate another hour before we get there. How about we stop in here for something to eat?"

The crew of the Sniffwhistle entered one of the local taverns. It was a simple place, and, surprisingly, not overflowing with people. They found a table in back.

"Ah," said the proprietor, "you have come here at just the right time to beat the noon rush. In only twenty minutes more you would not be able to find a seat."

"Good," said Captain Wilham, "we'll just have the special of the day."

"Very good. Today's special is roasted ham with beans, and tuna fish imported from the finest saltwater oceans of the most watery planets known to man. And we mix a special sauce from the blended remains of forty-seven different species of herd animal. It is most delicious."

"Sounds good."

"And what would you like to drink?"

"Milk."

"Very good."

In ten minutes the waiter brought out a tray full of food. And three glasses of milk. In ten more minutes the entire restaurant was packed.

"I like this place," said Liddia. "It has atmosphere."

"And they sure know how to roast a ham," added Tilman.

"Yeah," said Captain Wilham, "we should come back after we finish this job."

As soon as they had finished their meal and paid, the table was cleaned and another group took their place at it. It took a while to get to the door, but eventually they made it back onto the street and started for the hotel again.

About an hour later they arrived at the doors of the Libantan hotel, the second finest hotel near the spaceport. The finest hotel was actually in the spaceport. But most people didn't stay there. No one knew why.

Captain Wilham led his crew inside. He went to the desk.

"We're looking for a man named Forquat," he said. "Is he registered here?"

"I'm sorry," said the desk clerk, "I am not allowed to disclose that information."

"No, of course not."

"Hey," said a man standing a few feet away. "I'm Forquat. You're the crew of the Sniffwhistle. Yes, I know who you are. Come with me."

The man led them to the couch in the lobby, where he promptly sat himself down. He produced a small package and tossed it to Captain Wilham.

"Take this back to Zargo. It's his problem now."

The man picked up a local newspaper and started thumbing through it.

"Let's go then," said the captain.

★ ★ ★

After thirty minutes of pushing through the crowd, the crew of the Sniffwhistle were only ten feet from the doors of the hotel. The party raged ever upward in intensity as the afternoon hours encroached and the sun moved past its zenith. Time meant nothing to these people. Every square foot of space was a party, and every party was a main event.

"This could take a while," said Captain Wilham. "Where's Tilman?"

Liddia looked behind her, her long black hair whipping around. "He's gone," she said.

"Great."

"He was here a few minutes ago, John."

"Here, I'll give you a lift."

Captain Wilham sat the package between his feet and cupped his hands. Liddia put her hands on his shoulders and her right foot in his hands. As her head rose above the crowd she looked around.

"I don't see him."

"Ah hell," said the captain, letting Liddia back down. "Well, he'll just have to catch up to us. He's probably having fun anyway. Where's the damn package? I sat it between my feet. Great, it's gone too."

"Didn't you stick a tracker on it, John?" said Liddia, calmly.

"Oh yeah, I did. Should have stuck one on Tilman." He produced a small device from his jacket and looked at the flashing screen. "It's only five feet away. That could take hours to get to it."

"Quit complaining. Let's go."

They quickly forced their way through the crowded street with the package remaining just feet away.

"Looks like it went into that building," said Captain Wilham.

They pushed their way to the doors of a tee shirt shop, and sprang inside. A young man spun around; his hands wrapped around the package.

"I believe that's mine," said Captain Wilham.

"No, I found it on the street."

"Yeah, between my feet. Now hand it over."

The man looked like he was high on something, and started to make a wild dash. Liddia sprang out from behind a rack of tee shirts and took him to the floor. She punched him in the jaw and the young man let go of the package.

Captain Wilham walked over and put his foot on the man. "I'd stay down if I were you," he said.

Liddia grabbed the package and stood up.

★ ★ ★

"So how much longer are we going to wait for him?" asked Liddia, sitting in the comfort of the Sniffwhistle.

"Well," said the captain, "it's almost midnight—so another hour. Then we'll go after him. It took us three hours to get back, and you know how he is, it could take him all night."

The airlock light came on.

"Ah, there he is."

The tall man walked into the room. "Hey guys," he said. "Sorry I'm late. Got a little lost and distracted—also married, briefly." He grinned.

"You can tell us all about it later," said Captain Wilham, "Let's get this thing to Zargo."

Once in open space they were immediately confronted by a small spacecraft with its guns pointed right at them.

"Hand over the package," said the man over the comm-system.

"No," responded Captain Wilham.

Liddia threw the ship into some incredibly advanced evasive maneuvers. Energy blasts shot past the Sniffwhistle.

Tilman powered up one of the turrets. He fired, hitting the attacking vessel, causing little damage, but it was enough to distract them.

Liddia made the jump to hyperspace.

★ ★ ★

"Oh, wonderful," said Zargo Flingo, almost jumping out of his chair. "You managed to retrieve it. May I?"

Captain John Wilham handed over the package. "It wasn't that difficult," he said. "I don't understand why you couldn't just get it yourself."

"I'm rich," said Zargo, "I don't do anything myself. Now, I have transferred the appropriate amount to your cred-line, and you may go. I'm very pleased with your performance. Should I require your services in the future, I'll be in touch."

The little service robot escorted them back to the Sniffwhistle.

"I wonder what was in the package?" said Tilman.

"None of our business," said Captain Wilham.

The little robot beeped. "It's just a yo-yo," it said. "He collects them."

"Then why would someone try to shoot us out of space for it?" asked Captain Wilham.

"It's a one-of-a-kind pornographic holo-yo-yo," said the robot. "Very valuable."

"I see."

The crew of the Sniffwhistle boarded their ship and set off to collect what was owed them for the Farnooshian Blue Bush. They planned on returning to Cantor Prime as soon as possible.

Free Pudding!

The night sky was on fire.

Energy blasts streaked through the space around the planet like shooting stars. Defense Force fighters exploded like miniature supernovae, then disappeared into blackness. The invisible debris field this created was a hazard in its own right.

The Defense Force pilot dodged the energy blasts even as the debris from his defeated comrades slammed into his shields.

"I'm on the lead ship," he said.

"*Roger*," replied his wingman. "*I'm with you.*"

Blue-white streaks shot past their small fighters as they headed toward the largest of the enemy vessels. With their friends still dying around them, they pressed on. They had to, for they knew the fate of Pudding was in their hands.

Their first shots found their marks, and they came around for another pass. Again they hit their targets, but little damage was being done; there weren't enough fighters left to win. The order was given to surrender.

The battle saw the fall of the last great Pudding stronghold, the planet Terry, and the defeat of the Pudding Defense Force. The two best pilots were captured and taken to Tychonie, home of the tyrant, Wertle the Bad. It was a sad day for everyone—except Wertle.

Wertle was bent on the domination of Pudding in the universe—the whole universe, mind you, not just an inconsequential bit of it like so many before him—and now the last planet to stand in his way had fallen. There was only one thing left to do: hurt people.

Jack stood before his captor, bathed in the reddish light of the Great Meeting Hall of Tychonie. Next to him stood his wingman, Thermon, a formidable man, now shackled just as he was.

Wertle the Bad gazed heavily at the two men (not difficult for someone of his stout girth) and said, "The two of you fought bravely. And since you somehow survived my fleet's onslaught at Terry, I have brought you here to serve as examples to any who would stand before me."

Wertle's throaty laugh reverberated through the Hall.

"You shall be thrown into the Tunnels of Infinite Peril," he said, reaching for the chicken leg which was sitting on a small table next to his ornate throne. "There . . . you will meet . . . your doom," he said between bites. "Trust me when I say it will be a horrific fate."

Thermon didn't. He was about to inquire when Jack piped up with, "Yes, you don't need to spell it out for us. We will take your challenges in stride and come out of it victorious. Then we'll come after you."

"I doubt it," said Wertle. "I could kill you right now, but that would be boring. Besides, no one comes out of the Tunnels of Infinite Peril—alive or otherwise." Wertle waved to the guards.

Thermon and Jack were taken away.

Jack knew what he and his companion were about to face. At least, he thought, they weren't being dragged to the Caves of Unrealistic Horror. He wouldn't be able to face that, and he knew it.

Thermon, on the other hand, was blissfully unaware of the things he faced—that is, as blissfully unaware as someone could be when he knew he would probably die. But he was hopeful.

The guards led them silently along, down the long hall to the big door, over the footbridge, down a brightly colored lane, around a few corners, back down the same brightly colored lane, then took the door on the right wall. At last, they stood at the entrance to the Tunnels.

It was a rather innocuous looking setting, not much to see at all. Just a steel grate behind which was the mouth of a small tunnel that became instantly dark.

The guards opened the steel grate, removed the prisoners' shackles, and shoved the two men into the hole.

Jack slid down a seemingly endless slide. On some worlds people actually paid good money for a thrill like this. This wasn't one of those worlds—and Jack wasn't one of those people.

He could hear howls occasionally behind him, but only when he wasn't yelling himself. This was not an easy ride. While most of the tube was worn smooth, bits of it weren't, and the friction was generating a bit of heat as well.

Then Jack popped out into the light. It was Electro-torch-light. But it was light. He moved out of the way quickly as Thermon emerged from the sliding hell.

"Well, here we are," said Jack. He managed a slight smile.

Thermon smiled too, but not as slightly. "So, what do we do now?" he said.

"Well," said Jack, "this looks like the typical 'get shoved in a tunnel, walk to the end, but not before fighting off untold destructive mind-teasing traps and monsters and the like.' But you never know, do you?"

"I suppose not."

"Grab a torch, and a few loose rocks. We might as well prepare the best we can."

They gathered up some nice jagged stones, and stuck them in the pants pockets of what remained of their flight suits. Their jackets had been taken and given to two little orphan children of the Royal Court; after Wertle personally orphaned them. That's just one reason he was called Wertle "the Bad."

Jack took the lead, holding his Electro-torch above his head. Electro-torches are a curious invention of a planet of curious inventions: Fernatalintodunger, or Fataldung for short. Fataldung made some of the most seemingly ordinary and archaic items new and technologically up-to-date; yet exactly the same in appearance. "Nothing Radical" was their motto. They made two sticks that when held together in a certain way would start a fire. And a spear that could bring down a giant killer mole-skunk with just one throw. The Electro-torch looked exactly like an old wooden torch, but it glowed endlessly. It wasn't any brighter than a normal torch, however; because it was designed that way—nothing radical.

"Let's hope we don't run into trouble anytime soon, I need a rest," said Jack, just before the floor dropped out from under them and they found themselves in a pool of what they presumed to be water.

Thinking quickly, as quickly as they could manage, they dumped the rocks from their pockets and swam up. Their flight suits were waterproof as well as their boots, and were also designed to insulate them from the elements.

They floated and bobbed on the surface for a few minutes, surveying the situation. The pool was contained by a circular wall, but just above the waterline they could see tunnels heading off in several directions. Electro-torches illuminated the area as they did throughout the tunnels. Then Jack felt something brush past his leg. He looked at Thermon who had an odd look on his face.

"If you say something just brushed past your leg I'll kick your ass," said Jack.

Thermon remained silent, even as the giant one-eyed shnick dragged him under.

"A shnick!" shouted Jack.

Thermon and the shnick flailed about going above and under the surface of the water. Thermon had hold of the eye-stalk and was attempting a rare pudjitsu maneuver. Jack was rushing towards them with the torch.

"Die you lousy shnick. Die!" exclaimed Jack.

"Hey!" someone shouted.

The two men were too busy to notice.

"Hey!" someone shouted again, "Stop that!"

This time Jack noticed.

He had been about to bring the torch down on the back of the shnick when he froze. From one of the tunnels he could see a strange looking fellow waving and apparently trying to get his attention.

"Don't hurt him! He's just being friendly."

"Wha'?" said Thermon pulling on one of the tentacles that was wrapped around his neck.

"Simbial! Stop that! Let the nice man go. There's a good boy."

Jack and Thermon watched as the giant one-eyed shnick released Thermon and made its way over to the man in the tunnel. He petted the creature's head.

"Good of you to drop in," he said, grinning. "Sorry, it's the standard greeting around here." There was a pause as the man sent the shnick scurrying away with a gesture. "My name is Bill. It's short for Jofarbillilandry. You might be wondering why I'm not called Jofar, or Landry, or something else. Well, I don't actually know, really. People just started calling me Bill. No need to introduce yourselves, we know who you are."

"Uh-huh, well, just lend us a hand or something," said Jack.

Bill pulled Jack and Thermon out of the pool. He handed them a towel then led them down the tunnel.

"You must be insane to have a shnick as a pet," said Jack, as he dried himself off.

"Yes," said Bill.

Jack and Thermon looked at each other indicating they weren't happy with the situation.

"So," said Thermon, "you said you know who we are."

"We do, yes," responded Bill cheerily. "You are the last of the Defense Force of Terry. Sent here by the Great Confectioner to save Pudding."

"And who are you?" asked Jack.

"I am Bill."

"I mean the *we* in you."

"The we in me?"

"Yes, who are you with?"

"Oh! *We* are the Pudding resistance on Tychonie. We don't actually resist pudding; we are freedom fighters."

Jack got that.

"What's with the flashy clothes?" he said.

Bill was wearing a multicolored polka-dot jumpsuit of red and orange on white. His hair was three pronged, about a foot long, and orange. Thermon had noticed this peculiarity, but had had other things on his mind and didn't want to comment.

"Oh, these?" said Bill, tugging at his shirt. "We were a traveling circus, until Wertle threw us down here in the pit. Thankfully he threw the entire circus down here, so once we got settled in—training animals and such—we started converting our equipment to be battle-ready. It took a while. But look at us now, we're freedom fighters."

The three of them rounded a corner and their collective gaze fell on the biggest collection of circus tents and oddities they had ever seen.

Jack and Thermon were awestruck. People riding ten-legged animals. Animals riding ten people. There was a lot of riding. It was a busy place.

"For weapons, of course, we had to make do with what we had to work with," said Bill. He pointed to his belt.

"What's that?" asked Thermon.

"We call it the Seltzer Bottle of Death."

"Is that a fact," said Jack rather nonchalantly.

"Oh yes," said Bill. "It's quite effective. Come on, this way."

Bill led them to one of the smaller circus tents.

Inside, the light was dim, dimmer than it had been in the caves.

Bill pointed to the pillows on the floor. "Have a seat, someone will be with you in a moment," he said.

On the floor lay several brightly colored pillows in front of a small rectangular table. The table was just high enough off the ground as to be convenient from a squatting position. On the table were laid out some brightly colored handkerchiefs. A single glowing candle was in the center of the arrangement. Electro-candles were strategically placed throughout the rest of the room, providing the ambient lighting.

Jack and Thermon sat themselves down on the cushions. Bill made his exit quietly.

The two pilots sat there, alone. It was a nice quiet moment, something which they hadn't had for some time now. They didn't say anything to each other. They simply enjoyed the silence.

Then, after about two minutes, there was a small explosion behind the table, and a large puff of smoke billowed upward.

The two battle-hardened men jumped up and back, when they saw a figure appear before them. "Be calm dear fellows," it said. "Forgive an old man's dramatic entrance."

There, behind the small table, stood an old man. He was dressed in a long, flowing purplish robe. He was short, with a long white beard, mustache, and equally long hair.

"Do have a seat. No one will harm you here," he said.

Jack and Thermon sat back down.

2.

"I am Farnacle, the seer. I also act as the high strategic commander. Would you like a cookie?"

The old man offered a plate.

"Uh, no thanks," said Jack.

"They're very good," said Farnacle.

"I'll take one," said Thermon, reaching for the plate.

"We're fine," said Jack, looking at Thermon.

"But I want one."

"What the hell," said Jack, taking a cookie for himself.

"That's just fine," said Farnacle, taking back the plate and setting it aside. "Would you like some warm tea to wash that down?"

Thermon smiled, his mouth full, and gestured that he would.

Farnacle poured a cup for each of them.

As Jack sipped his tea he felt the damp chilliness of the caves drift away with the steam from his cup.

They all sat there for a while staring at each other, then Farnacle spoke.

"I foresaw your arrival long before you were captured," he said.

"Is that so?" replied Jack.

"Oh, yes. It was all too clear." The old man waved his hands about in a mystical fashion. "It was literally written in the stars, you see. You have been sent to us to help destroy Wertle, and free Pudding."

Jack looked at the wizard, visibly unshaken. Inside, he was also unshaken—though he didn't know it.

"Well," he said, "I can see that happening, I suppose. I certainly have no intention of just quitting and letting that evil bastard win. But I don't see how a circus troupe is going to defeat Wertle's battle-hardened war machine. And unless you have a way out, we are stuck here in these caves.

"You don't have a way out, do you?"

Farnacle pondered this, stroking his long beard lightly.

"Well," he said, "no."

Jack looked less hopeful.

"But you underestimate us," said Farnacle, raising his right hand with only his index finger extended, "as will Wertle. We have been preparing for this day for a long time now, as I'm sure Bill explained. And as for a way out, there are but a few trials left to overcome; then we will be free to attack Wertle's castle, thereby cutting the head off the snake—and, of course, Free Pudding for the universe!"

Thermon was still enjoying the rather large cookie. He sipped some tea as he listened.

"That's a pretty simple plan," said Jack. "It doesn't sound very plausible though. And what about the trials you mentioned. Why haven't you defeated them yet?"

"That is where you come in," said Farnacle, in that mystic tone of his. "Or, rather, that is your first task, as there will be many tasks ahead for you and your friend."

"But shouldn't you have figured out a way out of here by now?"

"As I said, the task is yours."

"Uh-huh."

"Now, come, we have much celebrating to do. And then you must rest."

Jack wasn't sure he had any celebrating in him at the moment or even anything to celebrate. He had been captured by the enemy, thrown in a pit, dropped into another pit, thrust into some sort of predestined position for which he wasn't certain he was adequately prepared, and now asked to go to a party. It was all just a little too much actually. At least the cookies were nice, and the tea as well.

"Say, what sort of tea is this?" asked Jack. "It has a very pleasant aroma."

Farnacle got to his feet. "It's a special blend of ratlig dung and creeper-fungus, with extra ratlig."

Thermon wished Jack hadn't asked, but got over it quickly. He didn't know what a ratlig was, and he didn't care, it made good tea, and that was all that mattered.

Jack was completely unaffected by the disclosure.

"There is a surprisingly wide variety of things to eat down here. Thanks to the Electro-torchlight and the various things Wertle has thrown down here over the years. Now come, we must get on with things."

The two pilots followed Farnacle out of the tent, presumably to attend the aforementioned celebration.

3.

The party was already well underway when the three men arrived.

Jack and Thermon were amazed. The flashing lights and the banging drums—it was all very impressive.

People were grouped together chatting away. Jack and Thermon went up to one group to see what the talk was about. As it turned out, the group they approached was talking about pies, and just what kinds of disgusting fungi made the best filling. It was shortly revealed that most of the conversations were about pies. Farnacle raised a glass and tapped it gently.

"People, people," he said, "enough talk about weaponry. It is a time for celebration and rejoicing." He stopped and pointed to the two wayward pilots. He continued: "Our heroes are here, and now we can save Pudding and be free to roam the universe entertaining the happy circus goers once more."

The people let out a roar.

Farnacle went on: "In just a few hours we will defeat the last of the barriers that stand in our way of leaving these caves. Then we will put our long-thought-out attack plan into action, and launch our assault on the Great Tower."

The people cheered, and raised their glasses high above their heads.

Bill shouted, "The Great Tower!"

The people cheered.

"That's the plan!"

The people cheered again.

Farnacle said, "That's the spirit. With a can-do attitude like that we cannot fail. Now drink and dine and enjoy."

And that's exactly what everyone did, for the next three hours. Though it might have gone on longer than that, Jack and Thermon didn't really know; they had gone to bed after three hours and stayed there until they were abruptly awakened.

"Whaa," said Thermon, as the old wizard Farnacle stood over him shaking him gently.

"It is time," he said.

"Huh?" said Thermon. "Time for what?"

"Time to face the trials," said Farnacle.

Jack said, "You might as well get up now. You don't want to know what they do if you don't."

"Okay, okay. I'm up, I'm up."

"Very good," said Farnacle. "I will wait outside the door." He stepped out of the tent closing the flap behind him.

Jack was slipping on his boots as Thermon wiped the sleep from his eyes.

"How long were we asleep?" asked Thermon.

"Not long enough," said Jack.

"This sure is a nutty bunch," said Thermon.

"You got that right."

Thermon got dressed and the two of them left the tent.

"All ready?" asked Farnacle. "Good, now on to the trials."

4.

"Whew," said Thermon, shaking his head, "I'm glad we made it out of that alive."

"Yeah," said Jack, "those sure were some trials."

"I told you that you were the chosen ones," said Farnacle.

The circus took up positions around the Great Tower. They remained hidden though, to their surprise, there were few sentries around. It was supposed that since Wertle had now conquered Pudding, he was secure in his position and no longer had any enemies that could threaten him. Either that, or all of the guards were inside for some reason. No one knew.

"All right then," said Jack decisively. "We go."

And with that the troupe charged into action, following their long-thought-out plan.

The sentries fell, one by one, as the freedom fighters neared the gate. The flying machines dropped from the sky as they were hit. The automatic gun turrets were taken out with well-placed shots. The gate was theirs.

The demolition expert was brought to the forefront. He set his cream-filled demolition charges and signaled for those nearby to get back. The explosion forced open the gate. And the dash inside began.

Jack and Thermon led the way as they entered the Great Tower. They met heavy resistance once they were inside, but they were undeterred. The pies flew furiously. Wertle's best guards fell with soggy thuds. Some of the Pudding resistance fell. Foamy explosions rocked the halls. Jack and Thermon forced their way through the mayhem—they had bigger fish to parboil.

The two pilots pressed on through the maze of halls that made up most of the interior. They could hear the cheers as the battle raged on—they were winning.

"Where the hell is the meeting hall?" said Jack.

"This way," said Thermon, pointing to a sign that read Meeting Hall.

"There we go," said Jack.

Out of nowhere, the guards appeared. They grabbed Jack and threw him to the floor. Four guards piled on Thermon. He smashed two of them into the wall, but the other two managed to take him down.

Jack fired his muffin shooter and one of the guards dropped.

The other guard pulled his weapon and started shooting.

Jack rolled to the right, and fired again. The muffin exploded against the wall. The guard had jumped to avoid it and hit the floor.

Thermon managed to knock one of his attackers away, but the others quickly had him restrained.

Jack tumbled with the other guard, wrestling for their weapons.

A scream of anguish came from behind him; he thought it must have been his friend, but he couldn't turn to look. Then he heard another scream that caused the guard he was fighting to be distracted just long enough. Jack fired. The muffin hit the man square in the chest; the blast threw him backward where he slumped in the corner.

Jack turned around to see what had happened.

There was Bill, his seltzer bottle in hand, standing over two writhing figures. Thermon dispatched the other two guards, who soon fell.

"I told you it was effective," said Bill.

Jack held up his hand and gestured they should move forward.

Through the double doors they flew, launching pies and flaming frothy grenades. Jack and Thermon had two of the guards' weapons, and were letting all who stood in their way have it with all they could muster.

Finally, they reached the meeting hall. They kicked open the door and charged through.

Wertle the Bad sat on his throne, tapping his fingers. Two guards on the inside of the door fell as the seltzer and pies hit them. Two guards stood on either side of Wertle, and remained motionless.

Things settled down somewhat, as Jack, Thermon, and Bill strode up to Wertle.

Jack said, "I told you we would come back for you."

Wertle just grunted.

"Tell your guards to stand down," said Jack. "You've lost."

"Have I now?" said Wertle, his voice full of irony.

"Yes," said Jack, "you have."

"Ah, so you believe," said Wertle. "But I still have one more trick up my sleeve."

Jack fired a single shot.

Heat grazed Wertle's arm, leaving a smoking hole in his sleeve.

"Oops," said Jack. "I missed."

A look of defeat fell over Wertle's face. Surrounded and with his guards disarmed, he surrendered.

Wertle was taken into custody, to be held for trial for his crimes against Pudding.

The people cheered. Pudding had been freed. The circus went back to being a circus. The four-legged woman married the six-armed man. They had three beautiful children—all of whom became mathematicians.

Wertle was eventually thrown into the Tunnels to play with the shnick, while Jack and Thermon returned to Terry to help re-form the defense force, and prepare for the inevitable attack from the next lunatic who thinks he can control Pudding—the uncontrollable.

The Adventures of Robby the Dingo and Jerry the Dickcissel

Robby the dingo walked along the edge of the highway. He had just escaped from a zoo a few miles back, and now he was out looking for adventure and excitement—plus something to eat, a place to sleep, and something dead to roll in. He was actually only half dingo. The other half was unequal parts German shepherd, something akin to a beagle, and who knew what else. The zoo wanted him for reasons never apparent to him. So, when he got the chance, he escaped.

This was fun—walking along, alone, with huge beasts zipping by. The large creatures didn't seem to notice him, so he just tried to stay out of their way. They sure were fast. Must be mating season.

Robby ducked into some dense shrubbery, poking around for something to eat. He could smell something in there. It was some sort of bird.

"Hey!" squeaked the bird as the dingo grabbed it in his mouth. "Wait a minute!"

Robby held the little bird in his mouth and thought for a moment. "Why?" he said finally, out of the corner of his mouth.

"If you spit me out," said the little bird, "I can help you."

"Help me what?"

"Help you find a much better meal than myself, and a warm place to sleep."

"Seriously?"

"Yes."

"Okay," said Robby slowly, saliva dripping from his mouth. "But don' ga blyin iwee."

"What?"

Robby spit out the bird. "But don't go flying away."

"Oh," said the bird. "I'm Jerry."

Jerry was a dickcissel (a black-throated finch), and a fine one.

"I'm Robby," said Robby. "Now, where's the food?"

"You see that big sign?"

"Yeah."

"That's a restaurant of some kind. We can get food from the back. They just throw it out. Can you believe that?"

"Wow, that's pretty strange."

"That's what I said, but it's good eatin'. Let's go."

Robby and Jerry went toward the big sign. They went around back and ate well.

"So," said Robby, "where's the warm place to sleep?"

"Those soft puffy things look warm. Try that."

Robby went over to the garbage bags and cardboard boxes. He walked around in circles three or four times, reversed direction, and finally lay down.

"This will do," he said.

"Great, I'll just go hang out in that tree. See you in the morning."

A short while later, the back door opened and a man stepped out.

"Hey," shouted the man, "get out of here you worthless mutt." He picked up a broom and swung it at Robby.

Robby jumped up and headed for the road, glancing back at the man still yelling at him. Jerry flew down from his tree.

"Hey," said Jerry. "You okay? Guess that wasn't such a good place to sleep after all."

"Don't worry about it. I'll just wander down this way."

A sharp sting hit his hind leg, and everything went dark.

The world slowly came back into focus as Robby opened his eyes. He was in a familiar place. It was the same zoo he had just escaped. He saw the two men that always brought him food and cleaned his cage. He noticed the people that always wandered by looking at him.

"Hey," said Jerry. "I finally caught up with you."

"Oh, hey," said Robby. "I guess this is it. I'm stuck here."

"Doesn't look so bad. I've been watching the other animals, and they all get fed and bathed. Looks like a sweet deal."

"Yeah, I guess you're right. They never did anything mean to me here. But still, I feel unfulfilled."

"What do you mean? Hey, why are you looking at me that way? Hey, wait!"

Robby tore off the little bird's head and spit the body on the ground. Then he rolled on it again and again.

He sighed deeply. "Ahhh, that's the stuff."

Morris the Male Prostitute

Part 1—*À Paris*

Upon a great fall from a second-story window—from which he was meaningfully hurled—Morris saw an unconscious green man on the street next to him. Good thing the guy was there to break his fall. Green face paint? Nothing too odd for Paris, he thought. He checked the guy's vitals—seemed okay. With that out of the way, and seeing as he hadn't been paid for services rendered, he decided he would simply take advantage of this opportunity. So he rolled the guy—taking his wallet and what looked like a nice, albeit eccentric, watch.

Morris wandered the streets of Paris until he came to his favorite noodle bar, *Pho King Delicious Noodles*, where he sat down for a quiet dinner.

"And what will you be having this evening, sir?" asked the waiter.

Morris quickly eyed the menu. "Could I have a bowl of noodles and fish parts?"

"Yes, sir," the waiter replied in a biting Parisian tone.

While eating, Morris wondered where he could get another job that required a male prostitute to pose for nude paintings. Posing, you see, was his specialty, and he quite enjoyed it—except for the occasional irate parent, spouse, or lover who would grasp him firmly and toss him on his ear. No, he didn't like that part at all. But you have to take the good with the bad, he thought, and the noodles here were quite good; he would often drop in whenever fortune smiled upon him.

The green man remained a bit of a mystery, though. There was a particular oddness about the unconscious fellow. He played with his new watch. It had too many dials and buttons to be practical. Just as well the guy should remain a mystery—he did pay for the meal, after all.

It was getting late, and Morris thought he should be getting home, but home was a long way off—New York, to be exact. He would undoubtedly have to "get in good" with someone who could pay for the trip. This wouldn't be hard; a lot of rich men and women could be found at the usual hangouts. It would all be a piece of cake.

To be fair, he told himself this same story every night. "A piece of cake," he would say to himself. In truth, it never was.

The street was dark, save for the glow of the streetlamps; the time was right to hit the clubs. Morris walked slowly along the dimly lit sidewalk. Then, out of nowhere, a light struck his eyes. He threw an arm over his face. He wondered if it was the police on one of their nightly sweeps. A moment passed, and he was able to lower his arm.

As his eyes regained clarity, he saw immediately ahead of him—bathed in the glow of the streetlamps—a group of six figures. They were dressed in black and white: white faces, black berets, striped shirts, gloved hands.

"Ugh," he muttered. "What now?"

One of the figures approached him, extending a hand to shake, then shaking it as if he had grasped an actual hand, which he hadn't. He then produced a small luminous card, seemingly from nowhere. A photo shimmered to life on it: the face of a green man.

Morris froze. He had to think carefully about this.

The figure pointed at the photo, raised his eyebrows, and pantomimed a scene: walking along, drinking from a bottle, being lost, limping and maybe a head injury, shrugs of confusion, palms out seemingly asking for help.

Morris took a deep breath. He'd seen plenty of mimes during his time in Paris, so even as novel as this moment was, it still hadn't passed his threshold of unusual.

"I haven't seen him," he said finally.

The mime looked dismayed, glancing left and right. The other mimes had gathered around a streetlamp and seemed to be praying to it, in total silence, and adorning it with invisible offerings.

Morris reached out and pointed down the street opposite the direction he was headed. "You might try that way," he said. He saw his new watch glint in the dull light—his eyes widened at the realization of his mistake.

The mime's eyes widened too. And before Morris could run, he found himself trapped in an invisible box.

Oh shit! thought Morris as he pounded on the box that shouldn't be there.

The mime called the others over, silently. He pointed at the watch, then at the photo, then at Morris. The group of mimes exchanged heated hand gestures and pantomimes of what seemed like accepting gifts from the sky. They nodded in agreement.

The first mime pointed at Morris again, then at the photo, then mimed walking. Morris got the idea. He was to lead them to the green man.

Suddenly, he was free of the invisible box, but now he was restrained around the waist by what seemed to be an invisible rope. He realized this night wasn't going to go well at all, and his threshold of usual was only moments away from being crossed forever.

He led the mimes down the narrow sidewalks of Paris, back to where he had been tossed from the second-story window onto the unsuspecting pedestrian. The green man was gone.

Morris pointed and mimed as best he could that this was the spot. The mimes weren't having it and tugged on the invisible rope. Then a noise was heard down the nearby alley. They peeked around the corner to investigate.

There in the dim light of a doorway was the green man, holding his head and muttering in what sounded like a phony French accent. "Damn religious field trips, *mon Dieu!*"

The mimes, with Morris in tow, approached the green man.

"*Sacré bleu!* My watch!" he said, eyeing Morris suspiciously. He held out his hand.

Morris knew he wasn't getting out of this one, so he removed the watch and handed over the wallet.

"Empty!" said the green man. "You little shit. You owe me a debt. Come along."

Once back out on the street, a light struck Morris again, the same light as before. This time he was absolutely bathed in it. The light was not from the street but from the sky! A loud hum split the night. Without warning, a massive disc of flashing lights loomed overhead.

A beam of light flew forth from the bottom of the disc. Morris, the mimes, and the green man rose into the air and into the disc of flashing lights.

A local passerby who witnessed the event exclaimed, "Putain de touristes!"[1]

From a window, the mimes waved goodbye to the Frenchman still cursing below as the spaceship climbed into the night sky and out of sight.

Part 2—Life as a Deckhand

Morris leapt out of bed as the klaxon sounded its morning scream. There was a klaxon for everything on this damn ship. A klaxon for breakfast, a klaxon for lunch, a klaxon for emergencies, a klaxon for sleep time. It was nightmarish, and yet, he got used to it. After three days aboard the alien spaceship, he was getting used to a lot of things.

He made his way to the mess hall, where he sat down for a nice bowl of what he liked to pretend was oatmeal. It undoubtedly wasn't oatmeal, but it was close enough not to worry him.

Captain Pierre Lafont, the green man, stumbled into the room, drunk, as usual, and sat down across from Morris. "*Bonjour! Mon ami,*" he said, reaching into the cabinet and pulling out a bottle of wine and two glasses. "And how is my favorite passenger today?"

Passenger? thought Morris. He answered only with a raised eyebrow and a questioning stare.

---

1. "Fucking Tourists!"

"*Bien, bien,*" said Captain Lafont, pouring two glasses of wine. He pushed a glass in front of Morris. "Drink up—it's going to be a busy day. We make landfall soon." He spoke with a comically overdone French accent. "I know we met under trying circumstances, but it's been a pleasure to have a Frenchman from the Holy Land on board."

"I'm not French," said Morris politely. "I'm American."

Captain Lafont shrugged. "A pity. Nonetheless, your familiarity with the Holy Land is uncanny. The mimes have been overjoyed with your presence. They believe it to be the second coming of the great influencer, or some such. I'm not very religious, to be honest."

Morris took a sip of wine and sat back. "I've been meaning to ask," he said wryly. "What's with the French accent? I mean, you're all obviously aliens, but you speak English with a French accent."

"Oh, that's very simple, *mon ami*. Long ago, the people of Garglegarglegikmay, where we're headed now, based our entire culture on *La France*, from your world. Well, everything except the language—because *mon Dieu*, it was too hard!" Captain Lafont laughed. He settled down and leaned in close. "You see, these mimes are very serious about it all, making an annual pilgrimage to the Holy Land—*La France*. Usually, things go smoothly, *mais* . . . here you are."

A sad mime walked in, got some oatmeal, and left the room.

Morris watched, then turned to the captain. "What is wrong with him? The others all seem so happy."

Captain Lafont poured another glass of wine. "Oh, that's just Barlowe," he said. "Who knows what these religious types are on about. Best not to question it." He finished off his wine, tucking the bottle neatly back into the cabinet. "*Alors*, shall we commence with the day? *Bien, bien.*"

Morris got up and headed to the bridge with the captain.

Meanwhile, Barlowe, the sad mime, made his way to the observation deck, where he sat with his oatmeal-like substance and looked out at the stars. The wonders of the universe touched his soul, but he was still sad. The painted tear below his left eye and the painted frown around his lips informed the world of his sadness, but no one really knew the depth of it all. Even Barlowe didn't know for sure. He only knew there was something missing. Something specific. And somehow, maddeningly, he couldn't mime what it was.

On the bridge, Morris was instructed to clean the navigation console. He snapped to it, as there were worse duties he'd been ordered to do. Things actually weren't so bad aboard the alien spacecraft. Plenty to eat, no need to hustle for anything—just work to do. Still, he missed home. He secretly typed in Earth on the navigation console, just to see if he could pull it up.

Captain Pierre Lafont sat in the pilot's seat fiddling with the controls aimlessly. He started singing a song in French, or at least it sounded like French. Morris understood enough to realize it was mostly random French words—strung together over a French-sounding melody. "*Amour . . . je t'aime . . . jus d'orange.*"[2] Only the chorus, which was repeated several times, seemed to make any sense.

____

2. "Love . . . I love you . . . orange juice."

"*Bonjour, ma petite baguette,*" sang Captain Lafont. "*J'adore le fromage avec toi, chéri. Les temps sont durs quand le ciel est clair. Beurre, bière et vin.*"[3]

Then the captain's voice fell silent. He had passed out again. Now was Morris's chance. He pulled up Earth on the navigation console and pressed the button marked *Définir la destination*.

A klaxon screamed.

Part 3—Land Ho!

Morris leapt to his feet and peered out the window. He saw nothing—which wasn't an unusual sight in the deep, dark reaches of outer space. That's where he was, after all, not in a nice bar in New York City. He would love to be in a bar anywhere at this point.

He had assumed the autopilot would remain engaged when he altered the destination and that the ship would simply turn around, but he now realized that was a poor assumption.

The spacecraft zoomed along, careening to the left and to the right, and then up and down.

The mimes rushed onto the bridge, which was quite spacious for a ship whose only crew was the pilot, and seeing the potential for disaster encased themselves in invisible boxes.

Morris had learned nothing about flying the ship manually during his time onboard. He turned his attention back to the console—so many buttons. He had no idea what to do, so he pressed them all—one by one.

---

3. "Hello, my little baguette. I love cheese with you, darling. Times are tough when the sky is clear. Butter, beer, and wine."

The ship's erratic behavior only became worse with each button press—it was performing maneuvers that would make even a contortionist jealous. After a few minutes of this, Morris's stomach had had enough and staged a coup. He vomited. Then he vomited again. Morris decided never to press any more buttons—well, maybe just one more.

As the button clicked, the craft did a spin and stood on its end, then took off like a shot.

The mimes in their invisible boxes bounced around the bridge utterly terrified, except for Barlowe. He alone was calm. In fact, Barlowe was smiling.

The ship seemed to have locked onto a nearby planet. In fact, according to the display, it was the ship's original destination of Garglegarglegikmay.

Morris looked at the ground that was coming up to meet him and noticed it was a pleasant shade of green. Well, it would have been pleasant had he not been in an out-of-control spacecraft rocketing toward it at five or ten times the speed of sound. The klaxon sounded a continuous deafening whine. On the bright side, he couldn't hear himself screaming—which would have just made him very nervous.

It was at this moment, with collision imminent, that Captain Pierre Lafont awoke from his wine-induced stupor. "*Sacré bleu!*" he shouted, grabbing the controls. With instinctive skill and deft handling of his wine bottle, he took control of the ship—and didn't spill a drop.

At exactly ten feet from the ground, the ship came to an abrupt halt. The mimes flew to the front of the bridge where they emerged from their invisible boxes, and feigned a variety of injuries as the ship gently leveled out. Barlowe jumped with joy and pulled on an invisible rope toward the back of the bridge as if fighting immense gravity. It was the first time he had felt like pulling on an invisible rope in many years. Then he let go of the invisible rope and mimed a backward fall, waving his arms frantically. He grabbed an invisible rope again, and proceeded to repeat the performance. The other mimes were bemused by his apparent amusement, but content in their companion's satisfaction.

Captain Lafont breathed a sigh of relief, then turned to Morris. "Did you do this, *mon ami*?" The mimes collectively pointed at Morris, who nodded. "*Mon Dieu*," said Captain Lafont disappointedly. "Come with me."

Morris walked with the captain down a hall to a small chamber. Captain Lafont directed he should enter. Morris did as he was instructed. "I consider your debt repaid," said Captain Lafont. "You're a menace. *Au revoir*!"

The green man punched in a code on the panel by the door. A hatch opened below Morris, and out he went.

As Morris fell to the ground, he casually noticed a small bird falling alongside him. He wondered if it had been the spaceship that had knocked the bird from the sky and felt bad about this. He deftly tucked and rolled with the skill of someone who had been tossed from many windows over the years—which he had been—and came to rest on the ground.

"Tweet," said the bird in a very friendly way, looking up from the ground next to him.

With a relieved passion, he kissed the ground and hugged the little bird.

The spaceship hung in the air for a few minutes before zooming off, leaving Morris to fend for himself.

The little bird attempted to fly away, but promptly dropped back to the ground. It was an awkward-looking creature, with its head a little too big for its body. It was blue with yellow-tipped wings, scraggly, more hairy than feathery.

"You must be hurt or in shock," said Morris. "Let me give you a hand if you don't mind."

"Tweet," said the bird, who seemed perfectly at ease as Morris scooped it up and put it on his shoulder.

"There we go," said Morris. "Now let's see what we have to work with around here."

He stood up and took a look around.

It was rather boring really, a bit of a letdown compared to what he had imagined an alien world would look like—green grass, brown trees, the odd blue tree. He headed off in the direction the spaceship had gone—toward the lower of the two suns.

"You need a name," Morris said, turning his head to the little bird, "how about Buddy?"

"Tweet," said the bird—which in its language, meant *My name is Darglefrund of the Seven Quarking Gaggles, but feel free to call me Buddy. What's your name?*

"My name is Morris." He didn't understand the bird's language, of course, and it was only a coincidence that he said this.

As Morris walked along, he couldn't help but notice how much the fields looked like the French countryside. Rolling hills, hedgerows, bushy-topped trees. He couldn't remember the name of the trees, but they were everywhere in France. Aside from the occasional blue tree that seemed to stand out like it was intentional, it was starting to feel more and more like a pastoral stroll he had once taken to find some relief from the hustle of the city.

He spotted a familiar-looking animal grazing lazily in the next field.

Morris shouted, "Look! A cow!"

As he walked past the cow, gawking at it like someone who'd never seen a cow before, the cow said, "*Bonjour, monsieur.*"

"*Bonjour, madame,*" replied Morris out of habit. He stopped. "Wait. You can talk?"

The cow looked at Morris, bemusedly, and said, "*Mais, bien sûr.*" She snorted. "*Et vous parlez anglais.*"[4]

The cow's accent was typical of the native Parisians Morris had encountered on a regular basis. Clearly, this wasn't a rural cow.

"*Je parle aussi un peu français,*"[5] said Morris.

The cow snorted again. "*Ton accent est à peine meilleur que celui des stupides habitants du coin,*" she said. "*Que fais-tu avec cette créature répugnante?*"[6]

"What?" said Morris, looking around, ignoring the insult to his accent. "*Quelle créature?*"[7]

"*L'oiseau.*"[8]

"Tweet," said Buddy sternly. The cow took little notice.

Morris looked at Buddy, then looked back at the cow. "This is my friend."

"Plop-birds," said the cow, "they're disgusting. They can't even fly properly."

Buddy flapped his wings, taking flight for a few feet, then dropped to the ground.

"See what I mean?" said the cow.

Morris picked up the little bird and put him back on his shoulder.

---

4. "But, of course. And you speak English."
5. "I also speak a little French."
6. "Your accent is barely better than that of the stupid locals. What are you doing with that disgusting creature?"
7. "What creature?"
8. "The bird."

"Well, since you're so amazing, speaking two languages and all that, can I ask you for directions to the nearest city?"

"Two languages? I will have you know I am fluent in seven languages. Just keep walking that way." She motioned with her head. "You'll come to a road shortly. Follow it south. Once you're over the hill, you'll see the city in the distance. *La Citée in La Distaunce*, they call it. *Imbéciles*."

"*Merci*," said Morris. "Uh, which way is south?"

"That way." The cow nodded her head.

Morris waved goodbye as he and Buddy the Plop-bird headed toward the road.

"Tweet," said Buddy, as one last retort.

"I heard that," said the cow. "Filthy creature."

Part 4—*La Citée in La Distaunce*

As the two fast friends, Morris and Buddy, neared the city, Morris watched in awe as saucer-shaped craft descended from the sky and ascended back up through the clouds. At a certain level, each ship would produce a beam of light before ascending—presumably picking up or dropping off passengers. Morris was starting to feel like he was made for this kind of adventure—how could he ever return to the humdrum existence of his normal life?

As they entered the heart of the city, cars flew overhead and passed by on the streets as pedestrians ambled about on the sidewalks.

Morris marveled at the architecture, which resembled a healthy mix of Gothic, Renaissance, Baroque, and 1950s science fiction. It was a lot to take in.

As he continued down seemingly endless winding streets, with Buddy resting peacefully on his shoulder, he stopped to say hello to the street vendors and other people, all of whom were green. They didn't seem to pay any attention to the obvious fact that he wasn't green. They greeted him graciously and had short conversations before going on their various ways. It was all very pleasant.

Soon, he realized, he would have to find a place to stay, if only for the night, whenever that was.

The city was abustle with activity. It looked like the type of place a person with Morris's talents could get a job and . . . wait a minute. Right then and there, he decided he would give up being a prostitute.

He laughed for a moment. What a ridiculous thought.

He dismissed it immediately and went looking for an opportunity.

He opted for the simplest approach, and took a position on a street corner.

Morris was only there for a short time before a short, stout man approached him and, in a deep, husky voice, said, "Uh, wudd ya like tuh pose for some nude artistry?"

"What?" Morris said dumbly.

"Ya know—paintins," said the man, "the kind ya hang on yer wall." His accent wasn't like the others—it was hard to place.

"Tweet," said Buddy, a little concerned.

"Nice pet ya got there," said the man.

"Tweet," said Buddy, which was Plop-bird for, *I'm nobody's pet, you filthy cur.* The fact that, so far, only a cow understood what he was saying was starting to frustrate him a little.

Buddy promptly fell off Morris's shoulder and landed with a thud.

"Yeah, sure," said Morris. "I'd be happy to pose for some artwork. What's in it for me?"

The husky-voiced man eyed Morris up and down. "*Deux-cents franc-crédit*. How's that sound?"

Morris scooped up Buddy, placing the little bird back on his shoulder. He didn't know what a "*franc-crédit*" was, but two hundred of anything right now sounded perfectly acceptable.

"Deal," said Morris.

The husky-voiced man led Morris up to the third floor of an old building. He flung open a door, and there stood a man dressed in a long brown robe with a big floppy hat. He had in his left hand a palette, and in his right hand a brush that he waved about meaninglessly.

"Hey," said the painter, "iss-a dis-a who you brung me to paint up all nice and-a pretty, huh?"

The husky-voiced man coughed, then replied, "Yeah, this's the one."

"Oh, goody, goody."

The painter was green, like everyone else, but had an Italian accent from an old movie Morris had seen.

Morris looked around the well-lit room. It was a typical eccentric-artist type setup, as far as he could tell—canvases and paints strewn about, easels and filthy drop cloths both on the floor and draped over paintings. He'd seen it a hundred times.

"Hey-a, you," said the painter, pointing at Morris. "Take off-a your clothes. We get started right away—chop chop."

"Tweet," said Buddy.

Morris removed his clothing and stood on the spot the painter directed him to. "It's fine, Buddy," he said to the Plop-bird. "This is what I do."

"Okay," said the painter, "why don't-a you turn-a to your left."

Morris followed the directions as instructed. He was very good at this sort of thing. This was his element.

It took several hours to finish the painting. But before Morris could get his clothes back on, three burly men with guns broke into the room.

"Okay, Jacko!" yelled one of the armed intruders. "Hand it over!"

"What is dis?" Jacko—the painter—exclaimed.

"You know damn well what this is," the intruder retaliated. "You owe the boss big."

One of the burly men looked down at Buddy, who was resting on the floor. "What do we have here?" said the man. "I think this might be worth something to the boss."

"Nab it," said the other man.

"Tweet," said Buddy, trying to fly away, but falling right into the burly intruder's hands.

"Got it," said the man.

Morris attempted to grab his clothes and get out.

"Where do you think you're going?" The man opened fire on Morris, who instinctively hurled himself from the open third-story window.

Morris yelled as he fell naked into a large trash bin, which was thankfully full of fresh garbage from the restaurant next door.

Landing face first in someone's former meal wasn't so bad— the food was rather soggy and provided a nice soft pillow for his tired head. But it was no time to nap. Morris struggled up and out of the trash bin and headed off down the alley, putting his clothes on as he ran.

The sound of more gunfire rang out in the night. Morris heard a muffled "Tweet!" Turning, he saw the three men get in a long vehicle, one of whom was clutching the small Plop-bird.

"No!" Morris shouted as the vehicle flew into the sky.

Morris watched the vehicle disappear behind the buildings. "That's my friend," he muttered.

The sound of police sirens could be heard in the distance. Morris decided it best to take off while the getting was good.

It was yet another job he got stiffed on—and they took his friend too. That's going too far, and this time he was going to do something about it. He had had quite enough.

Part 5—The Seedy Underbelly

Morris returned to the painter's room, which was in an almost undetectably worse shambles than before. "Where did they take Buddy?" he said forcefully. "And where is my money?"

Jacko, the painter, looked up from under his floppy hat as he sat slumped on a stool by a long wooden table. "Ah, is-a you," he said, shaking his head. "Go away."

Morris approached the painter, his eyes seething with ferocity. "I want my money, and my bird!"

Unconcerned, the painter stared at Morris for a moment. "Is-a okay then, I will-a tell you they took all-a my money. But if-a you want-a to find them, they-a will be at six-a twenty-a-five *Rue de Hor d'Oeuvre*." He wrote it down on a scrap of paper and handed it to Morris. "Now leave me to suffer."

Just then, the husky-voiced man rushed into the room, pushing Morris aside. He knelt next to the painter, consoling him as he sobbed dramatically.

Morris looked at the pair, then looked at the scrap of paper. Determination filled his lungs with the deep breath he took. He didn't know how he would do it, but he was going to get his new friend back. He left the painter and his assistant to mourn in peace, and out into the night he went.

Not knowing where anything was, he found a quiet cafe where he could ask directions. The waitress was very helpful, and he was off again.

Along the darkened city streets of an alien world, Morris made his way to the address of the kidnappers of his friend. It was a warehouse building, with two large garage doors, a smaller door, and several open windows. A guard was standing by the door, so he opted to enter through a window.

He silently climbed through the window, and found a hiding place behind some crates. He could hear a conversation going on, so he peeked over the crates, and could see several men standing around talking. On a chair, in a cage, was Buddy!

"So this is what you brought me?" said one of the men as he examined the bird in the cage.

"Yes, boss. It's a Plop-bird."

"I know what it is," said the boss. "But is it *the* Plop-bird?"

Buddy didn't say anything.

"We can find out easily enough," said one of the men.

"Indeed we can, Joey," said the boss.

"Mikey, run and get the papers," said Joey.

The man ran up to the office and brought back a newspaper.

Everyone stood around and looked at the newspaper, then at the Plop-bird, and back again. They paused and mumbled to each other, then looked again. The boss set the newspaper on the cage.

"I think it's him," said Joey.

"I'm ripple with that, Joey," said the boss. "Let's give 'em a call an' see what we can get. Mikey, watch the bird."

The group of men, except Mikey, went to the office.

This was the time, Morris thought. He looked around and found a length of pipe. With the stealth of a well-honed street-walker, he came up behind the man guarding his friend, and clubbed him in the back of the head with the pipe.

As the man fell to the floor, Morris opened the cage and held Buddy gently, but securely in his hand. "Stay quiet," he said. "We're getting out of here."

Buddy looked up at him and said quietly, "Tweet."

Morris noticed the newspaper on the cage. It looked like a picture of Buddy under the headline *Crown Prince Missing*. No time to read it all, so he snatched the paper while still holding the pipe and headed for the window.

Less stealthily than he entered, Morris leapt through the open window and ran down the street with Buddy, newspaper, and pipe in hand. He didn't look back, he just ran.

Finally, after running for what seemed to be all night, he found a darkened doorway to rest in. Morris fell into peaceful sleep, with Buddy resting on his chest.

With the dawn, Morris was awakened by the sounds of pass-ersby, but everything seemed calm enough. Then the police showed up.

Morris was taken to the station, and after several hours, was seated in front of an officer in a small room with no windows. "Ah, *mon ami*, this is your lucky day, it seems," said the police-man, in his light-blue shirt, tie, and kepi hat. "You're free to go."

"Where is my friend?" said Morris cautiously.

"You mean your *bienfaiteur*?" said the policeman.

"What do you mean benefactor?" said Morris, suspiciously.

"Didn't you read the newspaper you had with you? Oh well, no matter. The prince and his father are waiting for you outside." The policeman walked Morris to the door and pointed down the hall. "Out that door and to the right. *Au revoir.*"

Morris found his way out of the police station, and there by a long, silver car was a green-skinned man in a black suit gesturing for him to get in.

As he climbed in the back, he saw Buddy. "Buddy!" he said happily.

"Tweet," said Buddy, also happily.

"Prince Darglefrund says he is very happy to see you well and to buckle up," said the thin green-skinned, dark-haired woman sitting next to Buddy and another Plop-bird.

Morris hadn't noticed the others at first.

"Tweet," said the other Plop-bird authoritatively, as the car rose into the air.

"I am King Karnisiumputtrefony of the Seven Quarking Gaggles," said the interpreter. "You have been so very kind to my son, the Prince, and a very good friend, indeed. I wish to bestow upon you a gift, a mere token, to show my appreciation. If there is anything you desire, please, speak of it now."

Morris thought for a moment. It was a lot to take in. So many things flashed through his mind. He could ask to be taken home, but *where* was home really? Did he really have a life back on Earth? It was just one struggle after another. No, the old way just wasn't going to cut it anymore. Suddenly, he had a plan. There was an altruistic gesture forming in his guts. It was unfamiliar, but welcome.

"I have an idea," said Morris.

And with that, Morris and Buddy, friends for life, founded an institution dedicated to helping those who had suffered the same hardships Morris knew all too well.

It was called The Home for Wayward and Ejected Male Prostitutes.

Meanwhile, some distance away . . .

Barlowe, the once perpetually sad mime, sat smiling. He too had a plan. As he packed his things to leave the Order of the Mimes, the others gathered around him to wish him the best of journeys. They patted him on the back, without actually touching him, while one pulled himself along with an invisible rope, waving farewell.

He silently vowed to never give up the way of the mime, but made it clear the Order was not where he was meant to be. The others understood. They wished only the best for him.

And with that, he left the temple. On a street corner, at a bus stop, he sat and waited. He pulled a notebook from his pocket and began to go over his plan for the future. There were a few rough sketches of people clinging to bars while seated in carts, and others where they were being suspended by ropes attached to their feet as they fell from a great distance. Barlowe smiled. Written boldly across the top of the page was the name of his future park.

It was called *Amusement de Terreur*.

Conversations with a 4,000-Year-Old Fungus

In Carl Fornasagan's great and all-encompassing intelligence, he headed north in an effort to establish communications with a newly discovered 4,000-year-old fungus. The fungus, being several hundred acres in size, posed only a slight difficulty.

Carl Fornasagan approached the fungus with caution; he didn't want to frighten it. And squatting a few yards away from its edge, he said, "Hello there . . ."

There was no reply.

"My name is Carl Fornasagan," said Carl Fornasagan. "What's your name?"

Yet again—but with much more conviction—there was no reply.

"I can understand your not wanting to talk; being 4,000 years old, you've probably become very introspective—having seen many civilizations come and go. Well . . ."

Complete silence.

Carl Fornasagan continued unimpeded. "I suppose if you were in this particular spot all that time, you probably didn't see that many civilizations. But of course, that's not really my point."

The air was particularly sweet today in the resplendent locale of the Great Mold; Carl Fornasagan paused to get a good sniff of it.

"I bet you've noticed the change in the air quality. It was inconceivably clean 4,000 years ago, I imagine."

There was a stirring in the bushes as though the Great Mold were about to speak—but it was just a squirrel.

"What do you think has changed the most in your lifetime?"

Some scientist types were surveying something or other when they noticed Carl Fornasagan conducting his interview. "Hey!" shouted one of them. "Get outta here, you nut!"

"Well," said Carl Fornasagan, as the scientists charged him, "thank you for granting me this minuscule portion of your . . . oh, shit! Bye!"

And with the scientists hot on his trail, Carl Fornasagan bounded off through the woods and headed home—but not before tearing off a piece of the thing to keep in a jar in his closet.

And so goes what outlives man.

John Bonnell writes short fiction that is often satirical, occasionally philosophical, and not always entirely well behaved. His work has appeared in *Columbia: A Journal of Literature and Art*, the *Wisconsin Review*, and elsewhere. After a long absence from fiction, he has returned with a collection of stories that explore the absurd with a straight face. He also composes music and lives in Oklahoma.

www.ingramcontent.com/pod-product-compliance
Lightning Source LLC
Chambersburg PA
CBHW021214130726
47988CB00002B/655